LEFT
IN THE
WIND

LEFT
IN THE
WIND

THE ROANOKE JOURNAL OF

Emme Merrimoth

ED GRAY

PEGASUS BOOKS
NEW YORK LONDON

LEFT IN THE WIND

Pegasus Books Ltd.
80 Broad Street, 5th Floor
New York, NY 10004

Copyright © 2016 by Ed Gray

First Pegasus Books cloth edition May 2016

Interior design by Maria Fernandez

ISBN: 978-1-68177-126-7

10 9 8 7 6 5 4 3 2 1

Printed in the United States of America
Distributed by W. W. Norton & Company, Inc.

To Becky

LEFT
IN THE
WIND

PREFACE

If a tree falls in a park and there is no-one to hand, it is silent and invisible and nameless. And if we were to vanish, there would be no tree at all; any meaning would vanish along with us.

—William Fossett, 1754

The journal you are about to read is a work of fiction. It does not exist, even in the imagined form you find here. On its last page you will discover why.

But first you should know some history. Emme Merrimoth was an actual person, as were the other ninety men, sixteen women, and eleven children of the "Lost Colony," left on what is now Roanoke Island, North Carolina, in 1587 and never heard from again. Their names are part of recorded history, but little else is known of them.

They were left behind by their leader, Governor John White, who sailed back to England with several of his assistants and did not return for three years. When he did, the colonists had vanished, leaving behind the ruin of their fortified compound, the letters "CRO" carved in a tree, and the word "CROATOAN" carved into one of the posts of the palisade. "Croatoan" was the name, well known to White and his returning crew, of what is now Hatteras Island, a short sail to the south. But White and his crew did not go to Croatoan after reading its name carved in the ruins of Roanoke by the very people they had come looking for. Instead they sailed away, heading toward Hispaniola and then England, passing within sight of Croatoan but not stopping to see if the English colonists were there.

Why? No one knows. The answer, like the colony itself, is lost to history.

When White sailed away from his still-vibrant colony that first time, he carried with him a document signed by each of the adults he left behind, entreating him to return to England in spite of his own desire to stay at Roanoke, in order to secure relief supplies for the struggling colony. That document, along with other records kept in England, is how we know the names of all the lost colonists, including White's own granddaughter, Virginia Dare, born to his daughter Eleanor and her husband, Ananias Dare, just nine days before White left the new world.

White finally returned in 1590 with three small ships that he did not command. On August 12, the ships anchored for one night off Croatoan. The next day they sailed north for Roanoke and arrived three days later. There, they saw smoke rising. Assuming they would find the colony still intact, White and several others went ashore, but found only the abandoned colony, those mysterious carved letters, and the remains of White's own chest of belongings, including his maps and drawings, strewn about and ruined.

After searching Roanoke for several days, the group decided to sail back to Croatoan. A storm arose, driving them offshore to deeper, safer water. But when the storm abated, they didn't sail back to Croatoan. They simply left. The captains of the three ships chose to leave for the West Indies and then to cross back to England. John White died in England three years later, and no European ever saw any of the lost colonists again.

We know all of this because White kept a journal. It tells his own version of the story—the only version known to history.

Which brings us to this, the Roanoke journal of Emme Merrimoth. Read it for what it is: fiction; a speculation; an imagination of how one colonist—Emme Merrimoth—might have recorded her own version of the story, and what she then did with the journal after she watched from Croatoan as the English ships sailed away, taking her last hope with them.

This is her story. But it's also a question:

If a story gets told and no one hears it, is it still a story?

Ed Gray
Lyme, New Hampshire

one

Tonight Richard Tomkins has been trying to play his fiddle. More and more he has been doing this, always at night, going alone down the beach to solace himself with unrecognizable music that none of the rest of us can avoid, not even the Indians in their darkened villages across the bay. He never was very good at it and now he seems to be getting worse, making up tuneless sequences of the only notes he knows. But none among us wants him to stop, for the strange new fiddle is the only instrument any of us brought here to the new world, and his playing of it does at least silence the faraway whoops and wails of the natives. Our men say the shouts come from Wanchese's men, girding for another attack on us, but we Englishwomen think we know better. We think it comes from their women, lamenting so much of what has happened so far, fearing what might happen next.

How long have we been here? I no longer know precisely. Others still watch and mark their calendars, but I am not among them. It is late spring, May or possibly June; that much is plain without having to mark off the accumulation of days that have passed since we came here. And if it is June, then more than a year will have passed since we left our homes and came to the island of Roanoke in this new world—or, as we have all learned by now, to this very old one. It is a world not very different at all from the one we thought we had left forever behind us as we sailed away from Plymouth, each of us looking backward as the Isle of Wight slipped slowly below the horizon, taking with it all we knew of civilization—its comforting rewards, the blinding falsity of its promises.

None of that matters now. None of it has since the day we were left here, abandoned by the very men who had convinced us to come. What story they told upon their return to England, at the end of their despicable flight, none of us expects ever to know, but it could only have been a lie. For it was upon an even bigger falsehood that John White lured us here in the first place. What sort of man could have done such a thing, to his fellow countrymen, to their wives and their children? To his own daughter? And to *her* daughter, his own new-born granddaughter, born in this new world while he was still with us, while he could hold the infant in his own arms? Even among the savages who have finally turned against us, I have not seen such low character, such a base capitulation to fear and selfishness. Though the governor and his dismal accomplices have left us here to live or die on our own, without even the barest of necessities and surrounded by increasingly hostile Indians, we are, in my opinion, well rid of him and those who fled with him. But I always have been an optimist.

two

I had meant to keep a journal. Truly it had been my firm intention from the very beginning, starting in November of 1586 on the English calendar (by which some of the others still keep track of the days), when John White and his son-in-law, Ananias, had come by carriage from London to Chelmsford, seeking recruits for their new colony in Sir Walter Raleigh's Virginia. But I haven't kept the journal. I haven't even started it. That I have had distractions, that from the beginning of the voyage itself I have found myself more an active participant than the passive observer I expected to be, is no longer important. That voyage is, like so much else now, long gone and far behind. What needs to be done now is the telling of the story of who we are, of what has become of us, and why. And so I have finally begun that journal, recorded here on the few sheaves of paper I hid from the assistants when they came to take my baby and penned with some of the red dye left here by Wanchese and his painted men, when they came after that.

three

Wenefrid Powell came by today to tell me that there is to be a council in two days at midday and I am invited. I said it was brave of her to come here to deliver the message, but she said that her husband, Edward, had ordered her to do it. He waited by their boat while she walked up the beach to my hut. Only the married women are allowed to speak to me, and not all of them are willing to do so. She said that she was afraid at first, but after she had come inside and seen for herself that I was still dressed as an Englishwoman and had not turned into a savage, she felt more at ease. Still, she seemed relieved when I thanked her for the message and told her to tell the others that I would be there. I think she must be among those not fully swayed by the fearful accusations of the others. But those must wait for their natural appearance in this journal, much as I would like to refute them here.

At the council I expect them to ask me many of the same questions they asked before, so I will need to remember everything, even the things I have already forgotten. Tonight, therefore, I will write down as much of it as I can, starting with the voyage from England.

four

The first time most of us heard about the proposed colony in the new world was when Governor John White and his business partners made the rounds of London and the nearby towns, recruiting people to populate it not only with their bodies and souls but with all their worldly possessions, as well. In my case the opportunity came indirectly, through the Tilers and Masons Guild of London, and through Dyonis and Margery Harvey, whom I served as live-in housekeeper. I never even saw John White until the week we departed.

I was twenty-five years old, eleven years past girlhood and enjoying the fruits of my parents' only legacies to me: rich blond hair, a comely smile, and fullness of body apparently irresistible to the attentions of men, and a cheerful willingness to return the favors. Married at fourteen and already twice widowed by my twentieth birthday, I had lost three babies by then, too, God rest their innocent souls—one to premature birth and the others, a boy and a girl, to fevers in the first year of their lives. After the death of good Thomas Merrimoth, a stonemason and my second husband

(God rest him, too), I had not remarried, though not for lack of diligent suitors among the surviving members of his guild. I had instead come to the belated conclusion that my household services were better compensated when done for hire, and that men were considerably more attentive if delivery of my more personal favors was at my option, not theirs.

After making a series of poor selections, passing from the household of one guild member to another and serving as wet nurse, housekeeper, and sometimes both, I finally found an acceptable situation with the Harveys. Both were honorable and fastidious in their personal habits. Margery was moody and aloof, but not demanding in her requirements for my services. Neither, unfortunately, was Dyonis. Quite unlike his fellow guild members, he never so much as made eyes at me even when I tried to let him know I might be receptive, a turn of events that more than once sent me to a mirror to seek out signs of premature aging. But take the good with the less good, I always say. At least their house and garden were easy to keep.

Dyonis had a friend named Ananias Dare in the guild. Ananias was a brick maker and Dyonis a master stonemason. Together they had worked on the repair of St. Osyth Church in Essex County and held each other in high esteem. Ananias, whose wife, Elenora, was Governor White's daughter, had been named an assistant to the new colony, the second rank behind the governor himself. There were to be only a dozen or so assistants among the 250 colonists, and Ananias wished Dyonis to be named to the same rank. But in order to facilitate that promotion with his father-in-law, Ananias told Dyonis that it would be best for him if Margery were to become with child before we embarked. The governor, he said, had indicated a great desire to increase the population of his colony and an expecting wife would go a great distance toward Dyonis being named assistant. "I speak from experience," he added.

"Elenora is expecting, then," said Dyonis.

"The least I could do," replied Ananias. "In the service of the colony, of course."

I was cleaning the Harveys' kitchen while the two of them discussed the opportunity. I could see my master was deeply uncomfortable discussing such intimate matters in my presence.

"Mrs. Merrimoth," he said, "please leave us to discuss this matter in private."

"Don't mind me, sir," I said. "I'm long past the blushing stage."

"As we are both well aware, Mrs. Merrimoth. But please leave the room anyway."

Ananias smiled at me. We certainly knew each other by reputation, and a similar one at that. Prior to settling in with the Harveys, I had been viewed as a bit of prized guild property, and Ananias, a most handsome man, was well known to have sired more than one bastard child among his own housekeepers. I had already declined several of his discreet invitations to meet privately and discuss "opportunities."

"And of course," he said to Dyonis, with a wink toward me, "as an assistant, you will be entitled to bring along a domestic."

I turned away. I had dearly loved my own babies but was in no hurry to have another, thank you very much, and certainly not one from a man already married. Nonetheless, as I left the kitchen I suspected that my future had just been settled.

I was right. By the end of the year, Margery was with child and we were all three enrolled in the colony. In addition to my duties as housekeeper to the new assistant and his lady, I was also to be midwife and wet nurse for the infant when it was born in the new world. I looked forward to that.

The next few months passed quickly as we packed up the Harveys' household effects, dividing everything according to which things would come with us on the initial voyage and which would be stored for later passage once their new home was established in Virginia. Each colonist family was promised five hundred acres, and assistants would have first choice in the selection. Even I, as an unmarried female, would be entitled to an award of land, should I remarry once settled in the new world.

Finally, in April, we traveled by coach to Plymouth, where we were to board the vessels in which we would cross the ocean to Virginia. It was there that I finally laid eyes upon our leader, Governor John White, a tall and well-shaped man in his mid-forties with pale blue eyes and a well-trimmed beard that showed no gray.

On the afternoon that we arrived in the port city of Plymouth, our governor gathered us colonists into a meeting hall where he introduced us to an Indian from Virginia.

His name was Manteo. He was extremely tall and dressed as an Englishman. His skin was dark but not black like a Moor, more the color of brick maker's clay, and his eyes were almost jet black, as was his straight hair. He stood a full head above the governor and was by far the tallest man there. What struck me the most, however, was his ability to stand immobile, erect as a stone pillar and just as unmoving, a pose that he seemed able to hold indefinitely. I had not seen anything quite like it. Though he was dressed the same as any of our Englishmen, he was quite plainly another sort of man altogether. After being introduced, Manteo said nothing, just nodded his head and resumed his rigid stance behind the governor.

Three years before our departure for the new world, the men from one of the earlier expeditions had brought two Indians, Manteo and Wanchese, back to England with them. The two Indians learned to speak English, and the next year, they returned to the new world with the colony that preceded ours. Manteo remained friendly to the colonists, but Wanchese turned against them. When that colony failed and the colonists all came back to England, Manteo returned with them; Wanchese did not. By the time John White formed our replacement colony, Manteo, who now spoke fluent English and had adopted all the manners of an Englishman, had become his indispensable partner. In Virginia, he would be our staunchest friend. Wanchese would become our bitterest enemy.

There is much to tell about both Manteo and Wanchese, but if I am to try to write this chronicle in proper sequence, then I must put their stories aside for now. For the truth be known, their stories are now inseparable from my own.

The governor then went on to tell us something of the new world. I learned then that John White was not only governor, but a well-known artist, as well. On his earlier expeditions to the new world, he had painted many of the wild creatures and native peoples he had encountered, and on this day in Plymouth he had brought with him many of those paintings, set out on easels for us to examine. They were quite fascinating, especially his paintings of the Indians in their native costumes—or lack thereof. Most were near to naked and had painted various designs and emblems directly onto the skin of their exposed arms and legs, even the women, all of whom seemed thin and small-breasted, more like young girls than grown women. It occurred to me that this may have been because in every painting of an Englishwoman I had seen, the subject was fully attired in the several layers of garments that we all wore here. On the other hand, were John White to paint my own likeness in the state of undress enjoyed by his Indian women, no viewer would mistake this subject for an unblossomed child.

After we had looked at his paintings and he had taken some time to describe each one, Governor White then subjected all of us to the first of the weekly orations of which we were all to eventually grow weary.

"Children," intoned the governor in his deep voice, "hear me. We embark together on God's work, not only to establish a lasting colony in the new world, but to bring Christ's holy word to the innocent savages who live there." He went on in this vein for almost an hour.

His speech surprised me greatly, for I hadn't heard any discussion that our new colony might in some way be a religious undertaking. And the good Lord knew my own widowhood was no one's exemplar of His holy word in action. Truth be told, I was probably more in need of having redemption brought to me than were Manteo's kith and kin across the ocean, if John White's innocent likenesses of them were any indication.

After the oration, Governor White released us to begin stowing our possessions aboard the vessels. Though some in our company had been moved by the speech, I had my doubts. Men's protestations of grand intentions I had heard in some quantity, and long ago I had decided that most were a mask to hide the speaker's real purpose.

A week later—the first week of May 1587—we departed. As I watched England recede behind us, I knew that I would not grow homesick for London. I had no remaining kin, no others whom I would miss greatly, and some whom I would miss not at all. As I always say, every day is best viewed from the morning with anticipation, not from the evening with regret.

five

It must be nearing midnight as I write. Now the calling of an owl has made me long for the sound of church bells in an English village. I have been trying with some success to suppress such aching desires, but there are nights like this when I simply cannot. Audry Tappan told me just last week—or was it two weeks ago? Or a month? Time is losing its meaning for me—that Joyce Archard doesn't long for church bells. She actually hears them, quite as plainly as if she were still at home. They come to her, Audry had said, from all the way across the great ocean, calling her to vespers, and it's all they can do to keep her from walking into the water as she tries to answer them. Audry—who is still willing to talk to me, even if most of the others are not—had then looked at me, nodding her head intently, willing me to believe her. But she hadn't needed to: I knew it was true. Such things are happening to us all.

For instance: In the writing of this journal, I am beginning to sense that I may be having trouble discerning my dreams from reality. I am trying hard to separate them, but how can I know if I am successful? I write this question here because of what I am about to relate. I have no doubt that the incidents did take place as I am about to record them, but as I have said, I am beginning to have doubts about my doubts.

No matter, I will just write it as I recall it. What else can I do?

During the first week of the voyage from England, almost all the other colonists became violently seasick. I did not. I remained cheerful and unaffected in spite of all the despair and gloom that pervaded our cramped spaces below decks. My employers were poor company as they lay sick and complaining among all the others. While some of those not fully afflicted were able to provide a measure of relief to those in their households who had fallen ill, my master and mistress wanted nothing more from me than to leave them alone, a service I was glad to provide.

At night, not wanting to remain among the foul smells of the sick, I joined some of the others up on the open deck and marveled at all the sights and sounds that confronted my senses. As we rose and fell on the waves, pushed forward by the wind that whistled and whined through the rigging, our ship, the *Lyon,* creaked and groaned everywhere. Lines and ropes snapped and pulled, blocks and tackle rattled and thumped. The great canvas sails loudly flapped whenever they lost the wind and then boomed like thunder when they suddenly refilled, jerking us forward sometimes so forcefully that one had to hold on to something to keep one's footing. The nighttime sea itself hissed audibly as the sails pulled our heavy wooden hull through its black water, sending aside tumbling sheets of white foam that sometimes glowed with more than reflected moonlight. Phosphor, I eventually learned it was called, when I encountered it again in the shallow waters around Roanoke Island.

We colonists were allowed only on the main deck in the center of the ship. The high stern deck was reserved for Simon Fernandez, the master of our ship, and the rare few he chose to invite. Usually it was just his lone shadowy figure up there, barely outlined against the stars that seemed to rise and fall behind him as the ship rode up and down on the ocean swells.

For two nights I watched from the main deck while Master Fernandez held a round brass instrument against the night sky and looked at the stars. A wiry and dark-bearded man of about forty years who stood not much taller than I, as I knew from seeing him in the daylight, he was not only master of our ship, but also the pilot for all three in our flotilla. Some said he had been a pirate and had spent time in a Spanish prison for it and should not have been entrusted with all our lives and possessions, but none doubted his skills as a navigator. For myself, I found him fascinating. He seemed to know where we were even when there was nothing but ocean in every direction. I took comfort in seeing him up on the high stern deck, holding up his dialed instrument and pointing it in the same direction every night. As long as he was where he was supposed to be, then I supposed that we were, too.

Pirate or not, Master Fernandez was one of the few in our small flotilla who had been to the new world. Besides Governor White himself, there were only John Wright and James Lasie from the failed colony of two years before. And of course Manteo. The men from that expedition had come back to England not because the new world wasn't inviting or the natives friendly, but because their crops had failed and their relief ships had not arrived in time for the oncoming winter. Sir Francis Drake on his return from raiding the Spanish in the sea to the south had stopped with his fleet at the new colony at Roanoke, and when he learned of their plight, he had conveyed them back to England, leaving a small garrison of fifteen soldiers to protect what they had built there. That, at least, was the story we had all been told.

On my third night of watching him, Master Fernandez finally acknowledged me when he came down from the stern deck on his way to his cabin.

"Good evening, Mrs. Merrimoth," he said in his Portuguese accent when he was close enough to be heard over the ship's nighttime sounds. "I trust you are well?"

"I am, sir," I replied.

"And your employers, Assistant and Mrs. Harvey?"

"They are not, sir," I answered.

"A pity."

"I suppose it is," I said.

The hull creaked all around us in the dark, the wind rattled and thumped through the masts above. My hair kept blowing loose across my face and I kept pushing it back, holding it in place while the deck rose and fell beneath us, making me unsteady on my feet. He was not, standing with his feet well apart and completely at ease.

Sensing that he was about to take his leave, I made bold: "May I ask what it is you see in the night sky, sir?"

"Ah," he said. "The same as you, madam. The stars."

"But, sir, I am certain that I do not see them the same as you. It is said that you use the stars to determine where we are in this great ocean. Is that true?"

"You surprise me, Mrs. Merrimoth."

"In what way, sir?"

He didn't answer. Instead he just looked at me. I could see he was coming to a conclusion. "If you are here tomorrow night at this same hour," he said, "I will attempt to show you."

"That is most kind of you, sir. I will certainly be here."

"Good night, Mrs. Merrimoth," he said.

"And good night to you, sir," I answered with a curtsy and a smile, my hand still in my hair, holding it back.

The next night, as promised, he invited me onto the stern deck. He escorted me up the steep ladder and back to the stern rail behind the compass house where we were out of sight of everyone else on board. It was the only private place aboard the *Lyon* and it wasn't easy getting there; the stern deck was steeper than the main and the rolling of the *Lyon* was much more pronounced here on its tail end.

Once at the rail, Simon tried to tell me how to make star sights. Standing close behind me in the dark, he helped me hold the heavy brass astrolabe and sight along it toward Stella Maris, halfway up in the night sky. The rolling of the ship made it doubly difficult to keep the star in sight. I kept falling against him until he put his hands on my waist to steady me.

"With your permission," he said.

"We are all already in your hands, sir."

He continued describing the intricacies of his astrolabe, speaking from right behind my ear so that I could hear him over the flapping and booming of the sails. I leaned back against him and it wasn't long before his hands began to wander. This came as no surprise to me, even when he tentatively reached for the lacings of my kirtle and corset. When I made no move to stop him and instead continued to acquaint myself with the heft and feel of his astrolabe, he fully unlaced me, reached inside and proceeded to acquaint himself with the heft and feel of my unfettered bosom.

His loosening of my garments advanced rapidly thereafter, as did his exploration of what he found underneath. Only when I was nearly disrobed and he brought the loosening of his own breeches into the bargain did I put down the astrolabe and make an attempt to discourage him. What happened after that cannot be described in terms appropriate to this journal except to say that he was persistent and I soon stopped objecting.

Here, I think, I must consider how to relate an episode like this. Discretion and modesty dictate a minimum of detail, and good taste forbids the usage of the terms one might use in telling the tale where such anecdotes are usually shared, say, in a South Bank alehouse. Yet those terms and details can be critical to conveying the most impor- tant aspects of an amorous episode, especially when one of those specifics becomes important to the understanding of later events. It is a dilemma.

six

I have a solution: I will write what needs to be said about this particular episode, using the words it requires, on this separate sheet of paper. That way I can decide later whether to destroy or include it. Here, then, is a fuller description:

I can choose to remain silent while a man has his way with me as Simon did on the stern deck that night, but not if he keeps it up long enough to start me toward a bodily climax. When that happens, I turn vocal whether I want to or not, gasping more and more urgently until he brings me to culmination, at which point I often can't help but cry out loud as the ecstasy takes control of me. Neither of my two good husbands were very fond of this trait, for it let them know every time whether or not they were satisfying me, an accounting that declines over time in the best of marriages. Familiarity is arousal's truest enemy, is it not?

During my unattached widowhood with the guild members, however, this habit sometimes turned against me in an entirely different

16

way. Not every one of them who took his pleasure with me did so with my initial consent, as was the case with all of my employers prior to Dyonis. My subsequent attempts to freeze off an uninvited ravisher were effective only if I was able to maintain a stoic silence the first time he took me. But if the bounder was patient enough to draw me into the act with him and then to bring me to an obvious climax, how could he not but assume that I was thereafter his for the taking despite my protestations to the contrary? On that first night on the stern deck Simon brought me there not once but twice again before he let me go, and each time he had to clap his hand over my mouth, first to quiet my initial objection while he ignored it and shortly thereafter to stifle my appreciative response. Truth be told, only my resistance to the third time was genuine. It was near to dawn and I was exhausted.

This is most embarrassing to relate, I must say, these very personal things that until now have been known only to me and to the lovers who have known them with me. I have related it nonetheless because it is important to the story I tell. For as I was to learn later, Simon did indeed come to assume I was his for the taking, even after I no longer held the same view.

Back to the journal.

seven

Simon finally released me from his stern deck on condition that I return the next night. I curtsied, smiled, and said I would bend to his every order. Before going belowdecks I did not even bother to relace my corset. His loosening of it had been an unexpected relief. The next night I took it off before I came up for the evening's lesson, wearing just a single skirt and chemise with nothing underneath them. I've always been a believer in simplifying things whenever possible.

After a week, as other colonists began to recover their sea legs and the nighttime deck became more populated, the lessons came to a necessary end. It was unfortunate, for while I delivered my side of the bargain—quite willingly, I should add, and not in the most advantageous of positions, what with the rolling deck, the need to remain upright, and gasping for air behind Simon's various attempts to keep my expressions of pleasure just between the two of us—he had not yet fully met his side. I had learned that Stella Maris always lay directly to the north and the astrolabe's purpose was to measure its height above the horizon, thereby indicating how far to the south we had traveled, but I had not yet learned anything about how that calculation was made. His knowledge of me, on the other hand, had made considerably more progress.

Neither of us was to learn anything more from the other on the stern deck. For the rest of the crossing I ventured no farther than the main deck with the others taking the night air. Simon Fernandez continued to acknowledge me politely as he passed by on his way to the stern deck, but our shipboard intimacies, diverting as they were, had come to an end.

eight

We colonists spent much of our time on the *Lyon* in the overcrowded main cabin, where sixty of us were confined most of the time in order to make room for the working sailors above decks. The time was punctuated only by the governor's weekly hortatory on how blessed we were to have been chosen by the Lord to carry out such an important task, an hour-long ordeal we all learned to bear so stoically that our frozen expressions came to rival the stony-faced visage of Manteo as he stood beside his master and benefactor, glaring at us as if we were inferior even to him. After an uncomfortable and dreary six more weeks upon the great ocean, we finally saw the new world.

We came to an island in the Caribbean Sea with a name that now eludes my memory, passing strange and tropical in every respect. All of us colonists went ashore on a white sandy beach where the shallows were warm as bathwater and the sand almost too hot for bare feet. Birds walked nearby, unafraid, and all the trees and shrubs were adorned with bright flowers and nameless new fruits. The sun was so bright it made one's eyes blink. We walked upon the shore in a collective daze, so unused to solid ground beneath our feet that some of the others became seasick all over again, including my mistress, Margery, now in her seventh month with child. I tried to attend to her needs as best I could, but she would have none of it, ordering me out of her sight whenever I tried. Thus freed from responsibility, I was deliriously happy. If the rest of the new world was to be like unto this island, I could barely contain my excitement at the prospect of settling into it.

We stayed on the island for three days, sleeping under trees and glad to be free of the stultifying confines of the *Lyon*'s lower decks. There was fresh water to drink and in which to wash our rank, salty clothing. Some even made bold enough to bathe in the more private pools a short walk inland. Though I dearly wanted to, Mistress and Master Harvey would have none of it, commanding me to refrain from anything so risky as bathing in possibly tainted waters if I was to nurse their soon-to-be-delivered child. I was very disappointed, but what could I do?

Some of the others were incautious and ate of fruits that were unknown. They became very sick, but the maladies lasted only a day or two. Worst affected was Alice Chapman's infant, Jane, still suckling. When Alice ate of the fruit, the poison passed straight through to her milk and into the baby's mouth, whereupon it near to killed the poor little thing with a rash so red and fierce that none of us thought she would survive. Her all-night crying ran straight to my heart and I'm sure the heart of every other woman among us. I made a promise to myself to be doubly cautious when it came my turn to nurse Margery's baby, still two months from being born.

The plaintive wailings apparently carried all the way out to the *Lyon,* anchored away from the beach with John White and Simon Fernandez still aboard, for the next morning John White himself came ashore to inquire as to which fruit Alice and the others had eaten. When one of the company brought one of the angry fruits to him, the governor proceeded to make a detailed drawing of it. It was the first time any of us had seen him actually do the work of sketching and I, for one, was entranced. Several of us stood a respectful distance back and watched in amazement as the piece of fruit slowly appeared on the sheet of paper. When he was satisfied with the likeness, the governor packed up his tablet and pencils and returned to the *Lyon*. To my disappointment, Simon had not come ashore with him, nor did he at any other time.

After the island of the angry fruit, we sailed near to Puerto Rico, where we were told the Spaniards had a colony already in place. Simon Fernandez piloted us to islands that were far away from where the Spaniards might see us while parties from our ships went ashore to procure fresh water and food. On one of those trips, Elizabeth Glane's husband, Darby, failed to come back. The other men on that trip were quite agitated about it, saying that he had just run off into the interior and none of them could stop him.

None of us had gotten to know the Glanes very well. Darby was an Irishman who did not mix well with the rest of us English. As for Elizabeth, she was so taciturn and retiring that by the time her husband ran away on the island, none of us had so much as said "Good morrow" to her. No one whom I knew, that is. After we were settled on Roanoke, I would have a most unhappy exchange with her, but that story must remain untold until its proper time in this journal.

Governor White was very upset at the news of Darby's disappearance. He went straightaway to Simon Fernandez's cabin and the two of them disputed so loudly that their voices carried to the upper decks, though not clear enough for any of us to catch what was actually said, save for Manteo, of course, who stationed himself just outside the cabin door to make sure that none of us tried to interrupt. For the next several days our two leaders avoided each other; it was plain that the argument was nowhere near settled. The dispute cast a great pall over the rest of us colonists. We were totally dependent upon the two of them to deliver us safely to Virginia, and now they were at great odds with each other.

Our final stop in the tropics was at an uninhabited island called Caykos. We were there only one day and night, but in that short twenty-four hours my entire situation was changed.

The purpose of the stopover was to gather salt from the sun-bleached inland flats and to obtain fresh meat by shooting and gathering some of the many large white cranes that lived there. One of the assistants went ashore with a hunting party, and another group went to the salt flats. After they had left in their boats, Governor White approached my mistress, Margery, with, as he put it, a humble request. Might he have the temporary use of Mrs. Merrimoth, he inquired, for the purpose of having her wash some of his clothing? They were soon to meet the natives in Virginia, he explained, and as leader of the company he needed to be presentable.

"To the savages?" said Margery, ignoring Manteo, who stood just behind his benefactor.

"They themselves are quite presentable when the occasion demands," the governor replied. "As you shall soon see for yourself."

She then irritably waved her assent. A sailor was sent for the governor's sea chest and then he rowed the three of us—the governor, Manteo, and me—to the island. As we pulled away from the *Lyon,* I looked up to see Simon Fernandez watching from the stern deck. The governor looked in that direction, as well, and when he saw Simon watching, he smiled and tipped his hat. Simon turned away. Once ashore, the governor told the sailor to wait on the beach with the boat. Manteo slung the heavy chest of clothing upon his shoulder, the governor bade me follow them, and together we walked inland.

I was unsure of how to react. Before this surprising request, I had barely spoken to John White. Very few of us had. Apart from his weekly speeches and the display of his paintings, he had remained aloof from the rest of us colonists, meeting in his cabin only with the assistants, and not very often at that. On other occasions we had seen him talking with Simon Fernandez; those conversations were mostly disputatious. Now I found myself accompanying him and his constant companion into the tropical interior of an island. I scurried to keep up with the long strides of the two men.

Eventually we came to a small lake of fresh water surrounded by dense shrubbery and the tall trees that were called palms. Manteo walked to the shoreline, set down the chest, and immediately began to take off his English clothing.

"Sir!" I said to the governor. "What is he doing?"

"I believe, Mrs. Merrimoth, that he intends to bathe."

"In front of the two of us, sir?"

"In Virginia, Mrs. Merrimoth, as you will learn from the natives, modesty counts for very little."

Manteo stripped himself naked, left his clothes in a pile separate from the governor's, walked into the water until he was waist-deep in it, then dove forward and began swimming toward the other side. I had never seen anyone swim. I watched until he neared the far shore, perhaps fifty yards away, and then movement to my right caught my eye.

John White was now walking into the water, as well, fully as naked as was Manteo. I turned quickly away as he splashed into the water. Faint with embarrassment at what I had just glimpsed, I dared not look back. Our governor, as I had just seen, was a man among men.

From the water he said, "You came here to wash my clothes, did you not, Mrs. Merrimoth? So please turn around and get on with it."

I turned. He was in the water up to his armpits. I stared back and forth at him and Manteo in the water and then finally at the chest of clothing. I was nonplussed. "Sir, I have no washboard," I finally said.

"Then make do without one, Mrs. Merrimoth. But do get on with it. I should like to put something clean on."

So I got on with it. I emptied the chest of his clothing and dropped it all in the shallow water, then began rinsing, one piece at a time, squatting at the water's edge and swirling each garment back and forth before wringing it. As each piece was done, I spread it on top of a low bush so that the sun shone directly on it. When he saw that I had done a pair of breeches and a shirt, John White walked out of the water. I averted my eyes and continued working while he put on his clean clothes. When I could tell he was again attired, I looked his way.

He had retrieved his drawing tablet and pencils from the chest. He set them down and walked to a shrub, from which he plucked a small branch of flowers and leaves. Then he walked back to get his sketching tools, sat down with them, and began making a drawing of the branch. He concentrated fully on his sketching until I was finished. By then I was quite flushed and dripping perspiration. I looked across the water. Manteo had emerged on the far shore and was now turned to face us with his hands on his hips. His dark body dripped and glistened like a marble statue.

"While my garments dry in the sun," said the governor, still engrossed in his work, "you are free to bathe, as well."

"Thank you, sir, but my skirts are damp enough as they are."

"Then take them off."

"Modesty forbids it, sir!"

"Only for those still encumbered by it, Mrs. Merrimoth."

"And you believe that I am not, sir?"

John White continued sketching. "My son-in-law, Ananias, as you know, is a member of the Tilers and Masons Guild."

The flush that ran through me must have been visible. I quickly turned away before he could look up. "As was my good late husband, sir."

"God rest him," said the governor.

Across the way, Manteo had reentered the water and was swimming back toward us. I kept my eyes there, forcefully willing myself to regain my composure. If Ananias Dare had any reputation greater than his well-known one as a lecher, it was for the looseness of his tongue. God only knew what ribald tales of the willing widow and her employers he had related to his father-in-law.

"Is that why you brought me here, sir? To discuss the Tilers and Masons Guild?"

"Not at all, Mrs. Merrimoth. I brought you here to avail myself of your services as a laundress."

"And for no other services, sir?"

"None that come to mind, thank you."

He turned back to his sketching. I watched in silence until Manteo reached the shallows on our side of the lake, stood up in the water, and began walking toward the shore where he had left his clothing. He looked cool and refreshed as the water dripped from his body. I, on the other hand, felt unclean.

"Do we still have time, sir?" I said. "For me to bathe?"

"Of course. Go ahead."

"Would it be asking too much, sir, for you and Manteo to look the other way while I did?"

"False modesty is a sin, Mrs. Merrimoth."

So he had heard, and now he wanted to see. Had he chosen to look the other way and ordered Manteo to do the same, I would have quickly shed my garments and hastily splashed in and out of the water. But now, even though it sent my heart racing and made me feel light-headed, I forced myself to undress slowly. Gluttony was a sin, too, and if he wanted to commit it with his eyes, who was I to steer him on the path to righteousness?

Once I was fully disrobed, I took my things with me into the water until I was knee-deep. I rinsed each piece, then wrung them out one at a time before carrying them to the bushes beside where John White sat with his drawing tablet. I spread each on the upper branches in the sun, just as I had done with his. When all were thus laid out, I walked back out into the water until I was covered to my waist and dared not go any farther. I ducked down to quickly submerge myself, then stood back up and wrung the falling water from my hair.

I turned around. John White was still on the ground with his sketch pad. Manteo was standing on the shoreline, still naked. Both were plainly waiting for me to come back out of the water. I continued twisting and wringing my hair until it stopped dripping, then walked to the water's edge.

As I stepped out onto dry land, John White held up a hand. "Stay right there, Mrs. Merrimoth, if you please."

I stopped. "Manteo," he ordered. "Go and stand next to Mrs. Merrimoth."

"Sir—!"

"Be *still,* Mrs. Merrimoth!"

I watched in mounting trepidation as the naked Indian approached me. "Sir—!"

"Silence, Mrs. Merrimoth! Stay where you are!"

Manteo came and stood next to me. I barely came up to his naked chest. Quite agitated now, I stole a glance at him. He was not aroused. If anything, he seemed bored. He put his hands on his hips and looked away. I wasn't sure what to do with mine. I looked back at John White and decided to cross them beneath my breasts.

"Excellent." He smiled. "Now both of you remain still while I make my drawing."

"Of us together, sir?"

"Yes, Mrs. Merrimoth. Of the two of you. It is quite striking."

Undoubtedly. I cannot say how long Manteo and I stood side by side, both of us naked while John White concentrated on his drawing of us. I do know that it was long enough for me to grow even more uncomfortable. I began perspiring again. Manteo did not.

"Sir, what will you do with this drawing?"

"A fair question, Mrs. Merrimoth. Now please be still while I finish it."

"Sir, I must know what you—"

"Be still, Mrs. Merrimoth!" he said, quite forcefully this time.

After that I remained silent. I shifted my footing. Manteo did not. When John White finished his drawing, he put it away without showing it to either of us. "It's time for us to go," he said.

Manteo walked to his clothing and began dressing himself. I walked to where I had hung out the governor's clothes. They were dry. I began to gather and fold them.

"You may get dressed first, Mrs. Merrimoth."

I turned and knitted my brow at him. "I thought you told me that was a sin, sir."

He smiled and shook his head. "Our Lord was most generous when he endowed you, Mrs. Merrimoth. Most generous indeed."

I finished folding and packing his garments. While Manteo closed the governor's sea chest and lifted it to his shoulder, I walked to my own clothes and unhurriedly put them back on. They both watched until I was fully dressed.

"Mrs. Merrimoth," said the governor. "I would consider it an honor if you would allow me the privilege of taking your arm as we walk back."

"A privilege that I cannot deny you, sir."

He offered his arm and I took it as we began walking. Manteo silently followed.

"When we get back to the *Lyon,* Mrs. Merrimoth, I shall inform Assistant and Mrs. Harvey that your employment with them is terminated, that from now on your position in the colony is that of principal domestic assistant to the governor. You shall move out of the lower deck and into mine own quarters with Manteo and me. Does that meet with your approval?"

So many questions came immediately to my mind that I scarcely could enumerate, let alone address, them. I did not immediately answer.

"Your reticence is most becoming, Mrs. Merrimoth. I assume you are weighing your existing responsibilities against your enhanced future prospects."

"Indeed, sir, I am. Thank you for so concisely stating it."

"Not at all, madam."

"My first question, sir, is this. Does my approval matter, or have you already decided it?"

"Excellent, Mrs. Merrimoth. Excellent. The precise question indeed. And its answer is yes to both parts. I would hope to have your approval, but the matter is indeed decided. You will remove yourself from their household service and move immediately into mine."

"I see."

"Meaning you have reservations?"

"Sir, I am committed to be wet nurse to Margery when she delivers. I do not know that she has another option."

"An estimable commitment for which you are unmistakably qualified, Mrs. Merrimoth. I shall be happy to make that service available when the time comes. Have you any other reservations?"

I should like to be able to say here that I carefully weighed my answer, especially in light of later events, but the truth be told, discretion was not yet one of my assets. The prospect of moving out of the putrid and crowded lower deck and into a private cabin shared only with Manteo and the governor himself was overwhelmingly attractive, as was the prospect of later living in the grandest house in the colony. I gave it barely a second thought.

"None, sir," I answered with a light squeeze on his arm. "I am fully at your service."

Back on the *Lyon,* while Dyonis took the governor's edict with characteristic equanimity, Margery was more demonstrative, to say the least. Quite losing her calm, she shrilled loudly at Dyonis for not being more forceful in their defense, then at the governor for being an intolerable tyrant, and finally at me for being a disloyal hussy deserving of nothing less than being cast overboard. My own temper then rose—a rare occurrence—but before I could strike back with the multiple names with which I was about to describe her to the shocked colonists now gathered around us, the governor asserted himself.

"Take your indisposed wife belowdecks, Assistant Harvey, before she further embarrasses herself," he commanded. "When, and only when, she wishes to make a full and public apology to Mrs. Merrimoth, who is blameless here, will she be allowed topsides again. Do I make myself clear, sir?"

With the Harveys thus banished, the governor escorted me through the main door to the aft cabins, past the door to Simon Fernandez's master's cabin, and to his own door.

The cabin inside was smaller than I expected, barely deeper than a man is tall and about the same width. There was a small port high on the right side that could be opened or shuttered, and underneath it was a padded bunk. On the left wall was a small hinged writing table now folded up, and above that was another bunk, this one hinged and folded up like the writing table. In the corner was a small chair and, beside it, the governor's sea chest.

"Sir, there are only two bunks," I exclaimed.

"Manteo prefers the deck. You shall have the folding bunk to yourself, madam."

"I am glad to hear that, sir."

And so I quartered with John White and Manteo, though in reality Manteo was only part of our constricted little arrangement for that first night. And constricted it surely was. Glad as I was to have left behind the snoring and coughing dozens with whom I had previously shared a single, much larger space, at least in the main cabin I could get to my feet and move relatively freely when the need arose. Not here. I could not get down from my bunk without stepping on Manteo on the floor. Luckily, after that first night, Manteo moved to the passageway on the other side of the cabin door.

In the morning we weighed anchor. Although the weather remained tropically warm, the wind turned against us and we had to tack against it, slowing our progress. As was the ship's rule in times of frequent sail changes and course corrections, all but the *Lyon's* sailors were ordered belowdecks and told to stay there. Thus were John White and I confined to the small cabin while Manteo remained in the passageway, thereby guaranteeing the two of us not only total privacy but, because most aboard turned away from the formidable savage on sight, freedom from interruption.

John was sitting in the chair. I was sitting on the permanent bunk, looking down at him as the cabin listed noticeably to starboard and lurched awkwardly from time to time as the sea waves struck the ship almost fully abeam. We had closed our port to keep the warm seawater from splashing through and it was turning uncomfortably close in the tiny cabin. Had I been alone I would have started to shed clothing.

"Here is a God-given opportunity, Mrs. Merrimoth," said the governor.

"For what, sir?"

"An opportunity to draw you again."

"Oh. Yes, I suppose it is."

He opened his chest and retrieved his pad and pencils. "Please undress yourself," he said.

"You intend to draw me in the nude again, sir?"

"Yes."

"Are you quite sure, sir?"

"Quite sure, Mrs. Merrimoth. We are alone and will not be interrupted. It might even be more comfortable for you in this heat."

On what grounds could I refuse? I shrugged, stood up, and took off my clothes, laying each piece carefully on the bunk, bracing myself against the ship's unpredictable pitching and yawing while I did. When I was completely naked, I turned in the cramped space to face him where he sat leaning back against the downhill wall. I had to lean to my right and spread my feet to hold my balance. He held the pad in his lap as he studied me. A wave struck and I staggered forward, barely keeping my balance and nearly falling into his lap. I steadied myself and pushed aside a strand of damp hair that fell over my face. I could feel the fine beads of sweat running down my torso as he followed them with his eyes. He was perspiring, as well.

"How shall I pose for you, sir? The same as before?"

"Come closer, please."

I did, unsteadily. Now I was directly before him. He reached up with his finger and lightly traced one of the stretch marks on my belly, leaving a thin trail through the fine beads of sweat. I watched as he traced the others.

"Should you not be doing that with pencil and paper, sir?" I said.

He looked up at me. "You have been with child, Mrs. Merrimoth."

"Yes," I whispered. "Three times."

"And your babies?"

"All dead, sir, God rest their infant souls."

"God rest them indeed, madam. All baptized, I pray?"

"All baptized, yes."

"Then we shall join them one day in heaven, shall we not?"

"As I hope and pray, sir."

He leaned forward and brushed his lips against my abdomen. I was unsure what to do. He leaned back and looked up at me, then suddenly pulled me fully against him, smothering his face in my naked bosom.

"Sir, what are you doing?"

He began kissing me there. I tried to push away. He held me firm and continued until I stopped pushing back. Then he let me go and sat back. We looked at each other, breathing hard. We both knew how to play this game. Now it was my turn to take control of him.

"And how would you like me to pose now, sir?"

He stood up and kissed me full on the mouth while he backed me up onto the bunk and we fell down on it together.

He was—how shall I say this?—dominant. Afterward, as I lay enervated and recovering on the bunk, he dressed himself, then went back to the chair and picked up his sketch pad. I propped myself up on one elbow and watched as he drew my likeness that way.

For the next three days, except for calls of nature, we did not leave the cabin during the daylight, not even for food. Manteo brought that for us, knocking discreetly when he did. The rest of the time, we alternated between making love and making pictures of me. John White seemed driven to maximize his output in both endeavors. At night, needing a cooling down, we dressed and repaired to the stern deck, where we strolled arm in arm, much to the silent displeasure of Simon Fernandez, who assiduously kept his distance when we did.

On the fourth day, as John and I were in the middle of having each other again, he said, "Methinks I shall marry you."

"Excuse me, sir?"

"Don't stop," he said. "God has seen fit to put us together, Mrs. Merrimoth. Who are we to stand in the way of His plan?"

"This is God's plan, sir?"

"Verily. What else could it be?"

"Several other descriptors come to mind, sir." I emphasized the point, causing him to draw in a sharp breath.

"Yet I am persuaded that He desires me to populate my colony with mine own offspring. This," he said just as he finished, "is how I shall do it."

"Yes," I breathed a few moments later. "That is indeed how it is done."

When we both had our breath back, he said, "I shall want to marry you, Mrs. Merrimoth, as soon as we are safely delivered to Virginia. What say you to that?"

"What can I say, sir? In every way I know, I am already yours."

The next day we came out into the sunlight and resumed a more normal shipboard schedule. In conversations with the assistants and others, we maintained the appearance of a governor and his domestic assistant and they all responded with proper deference and civility. How much they surmised they kept to themselves. For the rest of the voyage, none said anything to me other than the occasional greeting they gave to any other colonist. Even Margery Harvey mumbled an insincere apology and was allowed back above decks, after which both Harveys remained aloof but polite. It was odd, and I began to wonder whether or not any of it—the stern deck, the island, or John White's cabin—was taking place anywhere other than in my dreams.

Meanwhile, at night as I looked at the stars, Stella Maris remained directly in front of us. We were at last sailing north, toward Virginia. That much I knew for certain.

nine

It must be nearing dawn as I write this, but it is still dark. My fire has burned down but it still casts a bit of light on this sheet of paper. The faraway whoops and wails of the Indians continue, as they have every night for two weeks. I've decided to be reassured by the sound, for our Englishmen who have fought with them say the closer the Indians approach, the quieter they become. When you hear nothing, it's because they are almost upon you. Their silence is frightening, and they know it.

But if they don't mean to frighten us, then why do they cry into the night like they do? Is it meant for us to hear, or something they do among themselves? Tomorrow at the council I must remember to ask Manteo. If he is invited, that is. But if they have invited me, then surely they will have invited him, too.

ten

After we left the Caykos islands, the next land we saw was Virginia. For several more days we sailed north along the coast, staying far enough offshore so that the land seemed to me and the other colonists to be little more than a smudge of low-lying clouds. John told me that we were looking for Hatorask, where we would be able to pass through the barrier islands and into the inland sea wherein lay Roanoke Island. He also said that Simon Fernandez was having some difficulty in locating the pass. That seemed strange to me, for I had difficulty imagining our pilot ever being in the least way lost.

Whatever the truth of the matter, on the third week of July we did eventually come to Hatorask, arriving late in the day, where we anchored outside the shallow pass through which only the smallest of our ships, a single-masted pinnace named the *Plumrose*, could safely navigate. Inside the pass, lying in a broad and shallow bay and still invisible to us in the ships, lay Roanoke Island. John's plan was to stop here long enough for him to go ashore to the island and confer with the fifteen soldiers left there the year before, and then to invite them to join us as we sailed two days to the north, where we were to plant our new colony in the great bay called Chesepiok. On the morrow he would go ashore for that purpose.

That night Simon Fernandez invited John to dine privately with him in the master's larger cabin adjacent to ours under the stern deck. John surprised me by insisting that I be invited, too. Simon graciously acceded and the three of us had supper. I put on my best gown for the occasion and took the time to comb and turn my hair into a proper bun and cap.

I had never been inside the master's cabin. It was two or three times the size of ours next door, and much better appointed. There was room for a table and six chairs, along with a chart desk and several built-in cabinets of drawers and a side bar with glasses and bottles of spirits. A single bunk was built into the port side, and along the aft wall was a padded settee. All in all it seemed quite luxurious, certainly so in comparison to the rest of the *Lyon*.

We three sat at the table and were served by a sailor who came up from the galley with each course, then exited without speaking. John began to discuss the details of his going ashore the next morning in the *Plumrose,* but Simon interrupted him.

"There is something we must discuss first, sir."

Simon then called out to someone waiting outside the cabin door. A sailor came in, very nervous and fidgeting. A thin, pockmarked man of about thirty years, he snatched his cap from his head and stood before the three of us, visibly shaking.

"At your ease, Codman," said Simon. "At your ease. Now please relate to Governor White and Mrs. Merrimoth what you have earlier today told me."

Codman was nowhere near at ease. It was hard to tell which part of him was in more rapid motion, his quivering jaw or his knocking knees. His poor hat would certainly never be the same.

"Sars," he stammered, "and mum. 'Tis about me friend Darby. Darby Glane. The one 'at run off on St. John island." He stared back and forth at us, like a stray dog caught in a pantry. He started to drool. Simon pushed his brass spittoon across the deck with his foot so Codman could spit into it.

"Go on, man!" ordered Simon.

"He's up to no good, sars. And mum. I fear it. No, I know it. He's gone and found the Spaniards, sure. He's gone and told them, sure."

"Told them what, my man?" asked John.

"'Bout us, sar. 'Bout the colony. 'Bout where we're headed, sar."

"And how do you know this?" asked John.

"Told me himself, sar, he did. Said he were paid in advance to do it, paid in advance by someone back in England, sar. Told to jump ship in the new world, find the Spaniards and tell them we've arrived. Wanted me to jump ship with him, sar—begged me to. And when I told him I would not, he told me it would be the death of me, sar, the death of me, sure. Said the Spaniards would do for us all. Would do for us all, sar! Then he just run off. Into the trees, sar!"

"And you did not stop him?"

"He just run off, sar. In an instant he were gone."

John turned to Simon. "How long have you known this?" he demanded.

"Codman came to me just today, Governor. You are the first to hear of it beyond myself."

John turned back to Codman. "Do you know the name of the place where we will found our colony? Tell me, do you know its name?"

Codman looked like he might faint. "Ch-Chesepiok, sar," he stammered.

"How did you learn that? It's a Crown secret!"

"Everyone knows it, sar." He looked wildly at Simon, then at me, than back to John. "Everyone on board, sar."

John was visibly angry now. "What else does this man Darby know?"

"What else, sar?"

John waved at the sailor. "Send him away," he said to Simon, who then dismissed the terrified little man. John put the fingers of both hands together and studied them. I could tell he was trying to control his anger.

"I expect you to have him hanged," said John. "The sooner the better."

"John!" I said. "He's just a—"

"Silence, woman."

"But he—"

"Silence!"

Simon leaned forward on the table. "He should not have kept that knowledge from us, it's true," he said. "He will be punished."

"He will be hanged, sir!"

"He will be punished, sir."

The two men stared at each other until John gave way. "The matter is yours to decide, of course."

"It is." Simon nodded. "And I will. Meanwhile, you and I must decide how to handle this new information. We must assume that the Spanish governor is by now aware of our plans. He will send a force to destroy us."

"Why would he do that?" I asked.

"Please remain silent, Emme," said John. "If you listen, you will learn."

Simon smiled at me. "The Spanish, Mrs. Merrimoth, have already claimed much of the new world for themselves. They have a large colony well emplaced already at St. Augustine, just a few days' sail south of here on the same mainland. They do not want an English presence here, and they will therefore, if Darby Glane is successful in announcing our presence to them, come looking for us. Should they find us, they will be able to send a great force to annihilate us."

"Is this true, John?" I asked. "Why were none of us told?"

"Master Fernandez paints too grim a picture," he answered. "The danger, if it exists, is minuscule. It was not worth the discussion."

It did not seem minuscule to me. And certainly it had to be worth discussion. But I caught my tongue. All it would draw would be another rebuke from John. He seemed quite agitated. "What is that you wish to discuss, Simon?" he demanded.

"Whether or not to proceed with our original plan, of course. If we continue on to Chesepiok, John, we will be placing the entire colony at risk. The Spanish know to look for us there."

John shook his head. "We have no alternative."

"Yes we do. We can deploy the colony here at Roanoke where one is already established."

John shook his head even more vehemently. "No! I will not have it. We are here solely to engage with Grenville's fifteen, offer them passage with us, and to continue north to Chesepiok. This I have agreed with Raleigh. The Crown has decreed it. I cannot change it."

Now Simon began to grow testy. "You most assuredly can change it, sir, and you must. As a shareholder and principal assistant, I demand that you do!"

John abruptly stood up and forcefully pushed back his chair. "You, sir, are in no position to make demands on me. This discussion is ended. Come, Emme. We are taking our leave."

"But—"

"*Come!*"

And so, abruptly, we left. For the rest of the night, John came and went from our cabin, meeting with the other assistants and selecting a party to go ashore to Roanoke the next morning. We barely spoke.

In the morning, John was in better fettle. He had appointed three dozen men to accompany him, armed and armored, and it was quite striking to see the change in the governor's demeanor when he was surrounded by such an impressive force of colonists now turned into soldiers. In groups of six, they were ferried over to the *Plumrose*, clambering aboard in the bright sunshine with a clanking of armor that we could plainly hear from a hundred yards away.

By midmorning all were aboard, including John and Manteo. The *Plumrose* weighed anchor, set the sail on her single mast, and we all watched as the pinnace passed through the inlet and into the inland sound toward Roanoke. I stood on the stern deck, and from this higher vantage point on the *Lyon* I could still see, above the low-lying land on either side of Hatorask Inlet, the top of the *Plumrose*'s mast with its bright red pennant flying gaily in the wind as it turned to the north and sailed toward Roanoke.

While I watched, Simon walked to the rail and stood beside me.

"An unexpected turn of events, Mrs. Merrimoth."

"With such an array to choose from, Master Fernandez, I am at a loss to conjecture which specific turn you mean."

He laughed. "Quite," he said. "Will you do me the honor of dining again with me this evening, Mrs. Merrimoth? I should like to discuss that array with you in a more private setting."

"I am honored again, sir. But I must defer the acceptance of your kind offer to the governor when he returns."

"He will not be returning, madam."

I turned from watching the disappearing pinnace. "What do you mean, not returning?"

"Precisely that. In private I will explain. Half after sunset, if you will. In my cabin." He bowed, turned, and walked swiftly to the forward rail of the stern deck, where he began issuing orders to the sailors down on the main deck.

What was this? I had heard nothing of the sort from John. I looked back toward Roanoke. The pinnace had disappeared. I looked down at the sailors and remaining colonists on the main deck. Nothing seemed any different. Here on the stern deck, Simon had turned to discuss something with one of his boatswains. His back was to me. I walked over and interrupted.

"Master Fernandez, I must know what you mean, sir!"

"At the appointed time, Mrs. Merrimoth," he said without turning around. "Now please leave the stern deck. I have business here."

Of course I left. No one hesitated when ordered from the stern deck, not even John himself. In a state of confusion and anxiety I went below to my cabin. For the rest of the afternoon I stewed over what Simon had said. John's chest of drawings and clothing was still here in the cabin. Obviously he intended to come back. But Simon had been so definite. Did it mean foul play? Did it mean something else entirely? From the small port above the bunk I watched as the sun slowly declined. It took forever.

At half after sunset, after dressing formally again as I had the night before, I knocked on Simon's cabin door. He opened it and ushered me inside, where his table was set for two, with a lit lantern, goblets, and a decanter of wine, and various sweets set out in anticipation of a later supper. Lovely as it was, I was in no temper for pleasantries.

"Now I am here and we are alone, Simon. Please explain."

"Make yourself comfortable, Emme. Allow me to pour you some wine."

It was the first time since the beginning of the voyage that we had been alone enough to use our first names with each other. Now, with my relationship with John standing between then and the present, it felt awkward, especially because the topic we had come together to discuss was John himself. I wondered if Simon felt the same. Watching him as he held my chair while I sat and then as he poured us each a goblet of wine, I could not tell. He remained on his feet, primed with energy as always, as truly tireless a man as I had ever known. I glanced at his bunk and wondered if he had lain on it even once during the entire voyage. I looked back at Simon.

"I am comfortable. And I am waiting," I said.

"You will recall our disagreement last night as to the proper disposition of the colony now that the Spaniards may have learned of it."

"Of course."

"Do you agree with John or with me? Should the colony proceed to Chesepiok or alter that plan and set itself up here on Roanoke instead?"

"Why does it matter what I think? It does not even matter what you think. John is the governor. It only matters what he thinks."

"What you think does matter, Emme. It matters to me."

"Why?"

"Emme, the colony will be established here on Roanoke. I have given orders to Captain Stafford of the *Plumrose* to leave John and his men on the island and to return here without them. As of today, the colony is formally installed on Roanoke Island. John White will not be returning to this vessel. The rest of the colonists and their equipment will be ferried ashore here, too."

I knew not what to say. So many questions came immediately to mind that none could find voice. Simon sat down opposite me, reached across the table, and took both my hands in his.

"Emme, I want you to listen to me. The colony is in great peril from the Spanish now. I do not want you to remain with it. I want you to return to England with me."

"I cannot do that. I am committed. And even were I not, Simon, I have no desire to return to England. There is nothing for me there."

"There would be me, Emme."

I laughed. "In what capacity? As my pilot? I've no need for navigational instruction in those waters, I can assure you of that. None whatsoever."

He smiled. "As I am well aware. But what I can offer is security, Emme. I can set you up in your own household. I am a man of some means. You will be more than comfortable."

"As a kept woman? Is that what you offer me?"

"You will be beholden to no one."

"Save you."

"Would that be so intolerable? How does it differ from your current arrangement with John White, save that with me you would be living in great comfort, safe from imminent harm?"

"It differs in one great respect, Simon. John and I are to be wed."

He certainly had not expected to hear that. "He has asked you to marry him?"

"And I have accepted."

For a long time he said nothing. "Let us dine," he finally said. "Afterward I want to show you something."

"Show me what?"

"After supper."

Soon the mess sailor appeared with our victuals. We ate largely in silence. At several points it seemed that he was about to say something but then he did not. In my turn I could think of nothing to say to him. I drank another goblet of wine, as did he. When our meal was finished, Simon stood.

"Come, Emme," he said. "Accompany me to the stern deck."

I shook my head. "All that is behind us, Simon. I am betrothed."

He smiled. "I just want to show you something."

Outside on the stern deck, night had fallen to full dark. The main deck below us was washed with the orange light of several lamps wherein several shadowy people moved together and conversed in low tones, and the *Lyon*'s great masts loomed upward from that faint glow, fading to black against the countless bright stars above them. It was quite beautiful, and it grew even more so as my eyes became accustomed to the night.

Simon took my elbow and escorted me to the stern rail where none of the lamplight reached. In the almost total darkness there, the stars above us came alive. I looked around until I found the seven stars of Ursa Major, then followed the end two to Stella Maris, just as Simon had taught me.

"Do you have it?" he asked, standing beside me.

"There," I pointed.

"As always," he said. "Now that you have north, turn and look to the west."

I did, taking a quarter turn to the left.

"Find the horizon. Look for its edge with the sky."

I tried, but could not. The sea was calm enough so that some of the brighter stars danced their reflections on the small waves, but in between them and the myriad fixed ones above there was an indeterminate darkness, a layer of pure black whose edges I could not discern. "I cannot make it out," I said. "It is just darkness. There is no horizon."

"What you are looking at and cannot see," he said, "is the land."

43

Of course. It was in that direction we had all watched earlier in the day as the *Plumrose* had sailed through Hatorask Inlet toward Roanoke, gradually disappearing behind the nameless barrier island until finally even the pennant-waving top of her mast had been swallowed.

He put his arm around my shoulders. "That darkened corpus, Emme, is the true Virginia to which John White has brought all of you. It has not the lights of London Town, nor even of the farm country in England. It has no light at all. That void, Emme, is your new world."

I shuddered with a sudden chill and leaned into his warmth, then quickly thought better of it. I pulled away, and as I did a strand of my pinned-up hair fell loose. I pushed it back. "Well, we are not in it yet, are we? I'd like to return to my cabin now."

Together we went below. In the empty companionway outside our two doors we stopped. My hair came loose, and again I pushed it back.

"Good night, Simon," I said. "Thank you for your hospitality and for your concern. But this new world is the one I have chosen, and it is the one in which I shall remain."

"And is there no changing your mind? You will not come with me back to England?"

"I am afraid not."

He touched the back of his hand to my cheek. "Then at least let me take the memory of you."

I put my hand on his. "That you already have."

"What I have is far from complete, Emme. Please don't ask me to make it last for the rest of my life."

"What more could you possibly want from me, Simon?"

"One more night."

"No."

We looked at each other. The loose strand of my hair fell down again, and this time I did not push it back. He took me in his arms and tried to kiss me.

"Simon, no!"

He opened his cabin door and pulled me inside with him.

"Simon, please!"

He closed the door and let me go.

"Simon, this isn't right."

"It never was, Emme."

He began to unfasten my gown. It was time to stop him.

"And how shall you pay me, sir? Your usual rate?"

"Pay you?"

"Surely you pay your other harlots. How much do they command?"

He stopped. I met his gaze and held it. He opened the cabin door and stepped aside.

"Good night, Mrs. Merrimoth," he said. "Sleep well."

"Thank you," I said. I started toward my cabin.

"Emme," he said. I stopped. "Forgive me."

I turned around, smiled, and touched him lightly on the cheek. "For what?"

"Thank you," he said.

We went to our separate cabins.

eleven

Since I started keeping this journal I have learned that writing helps to re-create details of events that I had thought lost to my memory. I think this happens because the act of penning events into English sentences is so much slower than simply thinking about them, or even than saying them out loud, the way the Indians do. I think this is because the pause to re-dip my quill pen after each word gives my mind time to search within itself for the next thing it wants to say. The problem for me now, as I try to enter into this journal all the events that have brought us to where we are today, is that all those recalled details are now becoming an impediment. There is not time to write it all if I am to bring this journal up to the present before tomorrow's council, or at least close enough to it so that I may be able to answer the council's questions. Though it is still dark, the daylight is already hinted at in the eastern sky. I have only a day and a night of writing left before I must begin walking to the settlement where the others live.

I am the only Englishwoman who dares to make that two-mile journey through the forest on foot, walking the path from my own outlying hut to the village. Just as Wenefrid Powell did yesterday when she came to tell of the council, any colonist who comes to call on me does so by boat or, if afoot, in the company of armed men.

Their caution is not unreasonable. Wanchese's men do sometimes paddle clandestinely from their village across the bay, and there is no doubt that those warriors would be willing to chance an attack on a lone colonist. But I have no such worry. Manteo's protection of me is known to all the Indians from all the villages, not just the Croatoans under his direct authority. How that came about is a part of this recounting that must come later, after I've described the important early events that transpired upon our settlement of this island.

twelve

When the governor and his men went ashore from the *Plumrose* on that first day, they set about immediately to make contact with the fifteen soldiers who were supposed to be living there since the previous summer. For two days they searched as much of Roanoke as they could, firing an occasional shot from a harquebus to make themselves known, the loud reports of which sent great honking clouds of water birds into the sky and carried all the way out to us on the *Lyon*. The shots were worrisome to me and to most of the others, but the more experienced men among the colonists and sailors told us not to fear as long as the shots were infrequent and evenly spaced over time. Those were signals. "When you hear an actual fight," they said, "you will know it."

When John and his party came to the northern end of the island, they finally found the abandoned and overgrown settlement of the failed colony; there was no sign of the men. All they found was a dried skeleton, too desiccated for them to know if it was an Englishman or an Indian, or even when and how the man had expired. They tarried just long enough to give the remains a proper Christian burial, in case it was one of the English, and then they retraced their steps to the beach. But when John called out to Captain Stafford on the pinnace, Captain Stafford shouted back that he had been ordered by Simon to leave them there on Roanoke. Then, ignoring John's thundering protests from the beach, Captain Stafford set his sail and returned to the *Lyon*.

Aboard the *Lyon,* all was a flurry of activity. The colonists had just been informed that we were all to disembark here at Roanoke. With John not there to look out for his own things, which were many, most of them stowed in sealed lockers belowdecks, I took on the job of locating and arranging for them to be transferred to the pinnace. Because I was unsure of the full extent of John's belongings and needed to keep looking for them, I chose not to be included in the first load of colonists to be ferried ashore.

It wasn't until I had packed up the last of John's and my things and seen to their transfer to the pinnace that I left on the last ferry trip of the day. As I and the last of the colonists were rowed away from his ship to the *Plumrose,* riding at anchor less than twenty rods away, Simon stood impassively on the stern deck, staring toward the open ocean and away from me and the others who were no longer under his command.

thirteen

My first week ashore on Roanoke Island remains a confused jumble
in my memory, even as I have tried to restore it to sequence for the
writing of this journal. No matter. The difference between one day and
another is unimportant. What matters is that we all set immediately to
the task of repairing the houses and outbuildings of the failed colony.

The men who had spent a year here on Roanoke had been diligent
in building their small community. Though we found it in a state of
disrepair, with the encircling palisade collapsed, the gardens overgrown, and the roofs of the English-style cottages porous and leaking,
the basic structures of nearly all the buildings were sound. It was not
unlike one of our country villages that had been abandoned during
the plague. I cannot speak for the others, but the disarray failed to
depress me. As I've always said, it's easier to clean an unkempt house
than to build one from scratch.

The governor's house was already there. Though little more than a
cottage by English standards, it was larger than the others. It was the

only one with a true second floor with sleeping quarters and its own kitchen shack; the others had low storage attics or no upper story at all, and shared common cooking facilities. John told me it had been built for Master Ralph Lane, the governor of the failed colony that had left here just over a year ago. It really was surprising how generally run-down the village had become in that short a time. Ananias and Dyonis, along with others skilled in the building trades, said it was because some of the structures were hastily built on fertile ground: Those structures had fallen more quickly into disrepair, and the natural vegetation had had most of last season and the beginning of the current one to reassert itself.

Those among us with some gardening skills, myself included, found the lush regrowth to be heartening. Perhaps we could grow some of our food crops this year, even though it was now July and well past planting time. While the men applied themselves to the heavier tasks of construction and repair, we women turned to the clearing and preparation of garden plots. The governor's house plot was already squared off and more than adequate for the needs of John and me, even taking into consideration that as governor he would frequently entertain others for supper. Since the others had to share several larger communal plots, I offered to share some of my plot with Margery and Elenora, but as soon as John heard of it, he said no. He chastised me for making such an offer without consulting him first.

After a week of this effort, our new home on Roanoke Island was greatly enhanced. All of the roofs were rain-tight and the cottages were livable, if not yet decorated. Wells were restored and new ones dug. The men now turned their efforts to restoring and building the more major structures: a forge and kiln, armory and storehouse, and the palisade around the entire village. We had been assured that the nearby Indians were all as friendly as Manteo, but in the name of caution against a possible attack by a distant, unknown band, self-protection dictated prudence. None of us were opposed, especially after what happened at the end of that first week.

George Howe, a gentle and good man who was one of the assistants and who had brought his ten-year-old son and namesake with him, set out with a group of men to catch some of the sweet crabs to be had in the shallows around the island. In his enthusiasm and concentration, George kept working his way down the shore while the others stayed together. Eventually he was out of sight of the others, and soon after that, they heard him cry out. Only then did they realize how far from them he was, as they could barely hear his distant shouts for help. They set out at a mad dash down the shore, but they could not find him. He had gone silent; now all was quiet except for the cries of wild birds and the gentle lapping of the waves on the shoreline. Searching diligently and calling out his name, they eventually found him. He was dead, shot full of arrows and with his head bashed in and crushed, lying half on the shore and half in the water. The men scooped up his dead body and rushed fearfully back to the village, keeping their eyes on the cedar woods along the shore. They never saw any Indians.

We were shocked and greatly dismayed. John immediately called us all together in the first council of our colony. We gathered in the newly roofed community building that the men had rebuilt from what John Wright and James Lasie said was the old guardhouse, the only structure large enough to hold us all. There were few chairs or benches yet, so we stood, save Margery and Elenora, who were very close to delivering. We left a space in the center for whoever spoke. John was first to do so.

By the time of the council we all knew what had happened. John said his purpose was to calm our fears, and he went on to say that he had discussed the incident with Manteo, and Manteo had said that the attack had not come from his own people, the Croatoans.

"How does he know that?" shouted John Nichols, one of the assistants.

"He knows his people," answered the governor. "He says they would not do that."

"Let us hear that from him," said Thomas Hewet.

John was incensed. "Are you questioning my word, sir?"

"Not at all, sir," answered Thomas. In England, he had been a lawyer. "But as we all know, our mother tongue is not Manteo's. It would boot us all well to hear the specific words he uses to convince us that his people are not our enemies."

John was not assuaged. "Sir, you have the specific words of your governor. Are they not plain enough for you?"

Thomas was not cowed. "They are plain enough, sir. But Manteo's would be more direct. I, for one, would like to hear them." This was followed by a general murmur of assent.

The truth was that very few of us had ever heard Manteo speak. In my almost three weeks of living in close proximity to him, all I could recall seeing were several short exchanges, none of any consequence and mostly out of my hearing. Manteo had no love of speaking, that much I knew. So it was a great surprise to me when Manteo stepped forward voluntarily to defuse the tension.

"Master Hewet," he said, "I shall be pleased to tell you in my own words." His voice was calm and firm, his accent apparent—more of an odd singsong than a mispronunciation of the individual words themselves—but no impediment to understanding him. He turned to John White. "With the governor's permission, of course."

John canted his head in approval.

Manteo then went on at surprising length. He first told us that his people were from the island of Croatoan, some two days' paddle by canoe to the south—he pointed in that direction rather than use the term—and that his mother was the queen of his people. A *"weroanza,"* he called her.

"Does that make you a prince?" asked Thomas Hewet.

"Not in the same sense as your English royalty," answered Manteo. "The entitlement is not solely by blood. It can be earned. But I and my brothers and first cousins, as you call them, have standing among our people because of the position of my mother. We are *weroances,* as are several other chief men in the community of Croatoan."

He explained that there were many towns on the lands and islands surrounding the great shallow bay in which Roanoke lay, and not all of the peoples from those towns were friendly toward one another. Wars were constant and terribly fought, and most towns had palisades around them in the same manner that our village here on Roanoke now had. The Indians who had killed George Howe, he said, certainly came by canoe from one of the towns across the bay, probably the one called Dasamonquepeuk, whose inhabitants had fought with the soldiers of the failed colony and whose great *weroance* Wingina had been beheaded by the English in one of their battles.

"The people of Dasamonquepeuk will always be our enemies," said Manteo. "We will have to be constantly on guard against them. My people on Croatoan, however, will always be our friends. Upon that you have my word."

Manteo's revelations were doubly discouraging to us all. None of us had been told by John White and his business partners that there were hostile native peoples in the new world, and we certainly had not expected one of us to be killed almost as soon as we had settled. Their painted picture had been far more pleasant, and as a result we were a colony of tradesmen and homemakers, not a garrison of soldiers. After Manteo finished speaking, several more colonists stepped to the center of the council to voice their displeasure. Eventually a consensus was reached: A group of colonists, led by John and Manteo, would travel down to Croatoan to meet with Manteo's mother and the chief men to learn the extent of the anti-English sentiment among the native peoples. John then asked for volunteers, and from the men's raised hands he selected twenty. After that, Manteo took John aside and whispered something to him. John then came back to the center of the council.

"Colonists," he called out to quiet the babble of conversation. "Manteo points out to me that in none of the previous expeditions to these shores have there been any English women. He says that his people have been told that all of England bears allegiance to our most gracious queen. Now they, and especially his mother, will want to see an English woman with their own eyes. So I will now ask for additional volunteers. Who among our women will travel with us to Croatoan on the morrow? The trip will take several days."

This was quite unheard of. Outside of our own households, where we might exercise some small dominion, we Englishwomen were used to being told what to do, not asked to volunteer ourselves for something this important. No woman moved to step forward. I thought I saw Audry Tappan make a tentative move to raise her hand, but her husband, Thomas, quickly pulled it down and said something sharply into her ear. When it seemed clear that no female hand was to be raised, I stepped forward.

"Sir," I said, "I will go."

"No surprise there," I heard Margery mutter from her front row seat.

None other raised any objection, but neither did any other woman volunteer to accompany me. So it was settled. That afternoon, John sent for the pinnace, and at first light the next morning we were under way toward Croatoan, sailing south along the outside of the barrier islands. The *Lyon* and the flyboat remained at anchor there, both ships still disgorging supplies, too distant for me to see whether or not Simon was at his familiar position at the stern rail.

fourteen

We arrived at Manteo's home island of Croatoan early in the afternoon. Like Roanoke, it was edged with a narrow beach of sand and covered almost in its entirety by a dense forest of cedars, oaks, and other trees whose names I have yet to learn. We dropped anchor and almost immediately some of the Indians came out of the woods, armed with bows and arrows and the short wooden swords some of them carried. Apart from Manteo, they were the first Indians I—and most of the men aboard the pinnace—had ever seen. They looked very much like the ones in John's paintings that we had all seen in England: tall and muscular, bald-headed on one side, and wearing only a bit of animal skin tied around their waists. They stood on the beach and waved their weapons in the air, shouting strange, high-pitched words in the same, singsong way that Manteo spoke English.

"Do they mean to fight with us?" John asked Manteo.

"That is how they demonstrate," he answered. "They mean to warn us away. I will speak to them as we approach in the boats."

Manteo did speak to them, calling out in their language as soon as the first boatload of us neared the shore. It was wonderful to see how joyously they greeted him, throwing down their weapons and running to surround him like a pack of children. He in turn embraced each of them while the rest of us gathered on the beach a short distance away. After the Indians had greeted one another, they regrouped and led us through a path in the woods to their town.

The town was like a primitive version of one of our own hamlets in England. Unlike some of the other Indian towns I would later come to know, this one on Croatoan had no palisade of tree trunks surrounding it, rendering the settlement far more peaceful-seeming even than our own newly rehabilitated one on Roanoke. The ten or twelve huts were rectangular with arched roofs, framed with tree trunks young and thin enough to be bent over and tied together. These frames were then covered, in most cases, with mats of woven reeds, which could be rolled up to let in light and cooling breezes on a hot summer day such as this was. The two largest huts were more like houses, roofed with tree bark and containing more than one room. In the center of this village was a communal fire pit with benches surrounding it, and surrounding the village were farm plots of corn, squashes, melons, and grapevines. All in all, it was quite lovely, I thought.

As we approached, a great clamor went up. Adults and small children alike came rushing from the houses and from the surrounding fields and woods. Soon we were surrounded with what must have been a hundred souls, each trying harder than the next to get a close look at us. Manteo shouted to them and they obeyed him almost instantly, parting to allow us passage into the center of the village. There, Manteo went to the largest house and stood outside its open doorway. His mother then came out.

I had expected her to be regal, though in what way I could not guess. And to me, she was, though not in the manner of our own Queen Elizabeth. Her name was Benginoor, and one's first and lasting impression of her was that she seemed always to be smiling. Like most of the Indian women, she was thin and graceful in her carriage, but unlike all of the others, she was covered above the waist. Her robe was a knee-length cloak of deerskin, fringed with pearls and dyed a brilliant reddish yellow. She wore earrings made of pearlescent shells. Her bare arms and the exposed parts of her legs below her knees were decorated with some sort of inking in the form of swirls and other markings quite unlike any I had ever seen. She was barefoot. Around her neck was another inking, drawn as if it were a necklace. Her straight black hair was cropped just below her ears, the way all of the women wore theirs, but hers was adorned with a wreath of woven metal—either copper or gold, I could not tell.

Manteo and his mother greeted each other by placing their hands atop each other's shoulders and touching their foreheads together. While thus embraced, they said quiet words to each other, then separated. It was quite touching, and it occurred to me that, when Manteo left for England the previous year, neither of them must have expected ever to see the other again.

Manteo then very formally introduced his mother. She welcomed us in a short speech that Manteo translated. After that, Manteo introduced each of us individually to her, starting with John as our governor and ending with me as the only woman in our delegation. Benginoor seemed very pleased to meet me, more so, I thought, than she had been with any of the men other than John himself. Later, when I had a chance to ask Manteo why this was, he told me he had told his mother that I was the governor's principal wife, a singular honor in their society.

"But, Manteo," I protested, "we are not even wed yet."

"By English standards, true," he said. "But here in our world, we do not have a ceremony to mark a marriage. It does not require an agreement between the two. A woman becomes a man's wife whenever he decides to take her as such."

"And if the woman does not want to be his wife?"

"That is of no consequence."

It had not been of much consequence between John and me, either, now that I considered it. On the walk back from the lake on the island of Caykos, he had told me as much. Now I wondered which set of rules he was applying when we became betrothed in his cabin on the *Lyon*. Would it have mattered if I had said no? Well, it did not matter now, did it? Events only correct themselves in one's imagination, not in the living itself.

The rest of that afternoon and evening were spent in feasting. A long woven mat was rolled out right down the middle of the main village lane and we all sat on the ground along its edges. The Indian women cooked and brought a seemingly endless series of dishes, served in wooden bowls from which everyone ate with their hands. There were stewed meats and vegetables; fish and crabs cooked over open flames; raw fruits and squashes; and diverse beverages, including sweet wine. Not all of it was palatable to me and the other new colonists, but John and, of course, Manteo ate and drank heartily of all of it. None of us left the long mat hungry, that much is certain.

That night, we slept on the ground, just as the Indians did, on woven mats under the roofs of the various huts. John and I were invited by Benginoor to sleep inside her house in one of the several rooms, which were divided by interior mats hung from the cross ties that ran from the exterior frame. The privacy was minimal, so when John seemed on the verge of waxing amorous, I told him that the strange food had given me indigestion and I was thus indisposed. No need to inform the entire household of just how principal a wife I really was.

The next day, our discussions with Manteo's people turned more serious. They told us that Wanchese, the other Indian who had gone back to England with Manteo the first time, had turned very hostile toward the English. He had spent the last year traveling among the various peoples who lived across the bay on the mainland, fomenting hatred against the white men who would come back to kill them all, as he told it. He now lived in the village of Dasamonquepeuk, just across from Roanoke, and it had been he and several of his cohorts who had paddled over and killed George Howe.

"Why?" asked John.

"The people of Dasamonquepeuk are afraid of the English," translated Manteo, after listening to several accounts. "They think they are not men and cannot be killed. They think that if an Englishman is killed, he comes back to life and fights again, so it is hopeless to take up arms against them. This they learned from Governor Lane of the failed colony, who was very warlike against them and who beheaded their chief Wingina in a fierce battle on the mainland. Before that, Governor Lane and some of his fighting men traveled far up a river into the mainland and were gone so long that Wingina believed them to be dead. So Wingina announced that Lane and his men had been killed by his warriors, and then rallied the other *weroances* of his neighboring villages to form a confederation and attack the remainder of the colony on Roanoke. But just before their planned attack, Lane and his men returned. The Indians, who had believed the Englishmen dead, now suddenly saw them come back to life. They abandoned their alliance and shortly afterward, Lane attacked Wingina's village and killed him. Thus was born the belief that the English could not be killed."

Manteo paused while he heard further details in his language, and then he continued in English.

"Wanchese, of course, knew that the English were men, the same as the Indians. But as long as the Indians believed the myth of the deathless Englishmen, he could not rally them to oppose the colony that you have now started on Roanoke. So to disprove the myth, he chose the bravest among the warriors of Dasamonquepeuk and paddled to Roanoke in the night, then awaited a chance to ambush an Englishman. Your master Howe was that unlucky man. That is why they so thoroughly killed him, by shooting him with many arrows and then by splitting open his head. Wanchese wanted his men to see that the inside of an Englishman is the same as the inside of an Indian."

There followed a great deal of discussion among all the men, English and Croatoan. The men of Croatoan, backed vehemently by Benginoor and Manteo, expressed nothing but solidarity and friendship with us. This was well received by our men. Manteo then asked the other *weroances* whether or not the peoples of other towns across the bay would be of the same opinion. There followed much discussion, the consensus being that the Croatoan men did not know. Benginoor then ordered several of her chief men to set out to the three nearest towns and tell them to each send a delegation to meet with Manteo and the English at Roanoke in one week's time.

Captain Stafford, who had been here with Governor Lane's failed colony and who had fought with Wingina's men in Dasamonquepeuk, wanted to know if the Croatoan emissaries were to go to that town, too.

"No," answered Manteo. "That town is now controlled by Wanchese. We already know that they are against us both."

John, Captain Stafford, and several of our men then tried to convince the Croatoans to ally with us and mount an armed campaign against Wanchese and his followers. This attempt was met with stoic silence. Manteo then explained that none of the Croatoan *weroances* wanted to add to the already existing animosity between their people and Wanchese's. It was enough, he said, that they had agreed to send emissaries to those towns whose intentions were unknown. This infuriated John.

"Manteo," he commanded, "tell your people that if they are to be our friends and allies, then they must join us in defeating our common enemy."

For a long moment Manteo did not answer. This angered John further.

"Manteo!" he thundered. "I command you to relate my words!"

Manteo stood. He turned slowly to face John who, like everyone else at the parley, was sitting on the ground. "Sir," he said gravely, "in this place, and before these people, you do not command me."

John came instantly to his feet. His face was flushed with anger. His fists were clenched. "Are you questioning my authority here?" he demanded.

Manteo remained calm. "Sir," he replied, "in this place, you have no authority."

I thought John might fall down. I had never seen him anywhere near this angry. But what I saw in him now was more than that. I thought I could see fear. He had never shown that before. He turned away from Manteo to face the rest of us English.

"Our business here is concluded," he said through clenched teeth. "To the pinnace!"

He turned on his heel and strode away. Of course we had no choice but to follow him, though it was immediately clear to me that many of the others were not happy with the manner in which our leader had comported himself. Nor was I. Manteo's people were our friends. Wanchese's were our enemies. What good could come of this outburst of wounded pride by our governor? I hurried to catch up to him.

"John, wait!" I said. He did not slow. "John, please! This is not right!"

He stopped and spun to face me. "Not right? I have just been disrespected by a savage and now I am to be lectured by a woman, and a guileless wanton at that? I will not hear it!"

The sensation was physical. I stopped and stood, reeling. It felt as though I had been slapped. He looked past me to the others who had now stopped in the path behind me.

"And I will hear none more from any of you, either! I am your governor!" He turned and continued toward the beach. The others followed, flowing around me as I began to cry. The others continued down the path.

I turned to look behind me. The village of Croatoan was out of sight. Manteo had remained with his people. I turned back. Ahead, the other colonists were about to disappear. I took a breath, banished my crying, and followed them.

What else could I do?

fifteen

For the next several days after the unfortunate events on Croatoan, there was tension not only between John and me, but also throughout the colony, as word of the governor's outburst quickly spread. Manteo returned by canoe on the third day, accompanied by an Indian man-servant who proceeded to erect a native-style hut for him a pair of miles down the shoreline from our English town. John and Manteo met privately, where no one could overhear them, and afterward their relations seemed restored. I, for one, could see no lingering animosity between them as they went about their business as before, the way domestic dogs, even after a snarling fight for dominance, will share a water bowl and curl up peaceably together as if nothing had happened.

As for me, I wasn't about to curl up peaceably until I got the apology I was owed. Thus, John and I no longer kept company. Though we shared the same roof, we spoke little and did not sleep together. Each of us went about our portion of the hard and busy work of building the colony, starting at first light and continuing until well

63

after dark, essentially ignoring each other. John met almost continuously with Manteo, Captain Stafford, and several of the assistants as they formed contingency plans to defend us against Wanchese's men. Meanwhile, I threw myself wholeheartedly into the kind of work I knew best.

Because none of us colonists had a finished home yet, meals were cooked and shared commonly, a task to which I devoted myself with a diligence beyond what was expected of just one person. In that process, I became much better acquainted with the other women in the colony, particularly Audry Tappan, whom I remembered for having been the one other woman who had wanted to accompany the men to Manteo's village. One of our daily tasks together was to scrape the scales off fresh-caught fish, a tedious job that required some attention to keep from accidentally scraping off some of one's own skin, but not so consuming as to preclude conversation.

Audry was not one to remain silent while she worked, or at most other times, truth be told, and most of what she had to say was critical of what she called the "unfinished thinking" of most people on most topics. She had been a tutor for many years in the employ of a well-to-do merchant family in the Midlands—Newcastle-under-Lyme, to be precise—and had not married until she was past her childbearing years. I guessed she was in her midforties. She was fixed in her opinions.

It turned out that I had been right in guessing that she had wanted to volunteer to go to Croatoan. Her husband, Thomas, had indeed pulled down her hand and forbade her from pursuing it. As she explained during the fish-scraping, she had only wanted to go so that she could hear for herself what Manteo's people had to say. "Translation is hard enough from one language to another," she said. "But a message loses even more of its verity if the words pass through an inferior mind on their way to an adequate one."

"And whose mind do you see as inadequate?" I asked. "Manteo's?"

"Of course not," she snapped. "He seems superior in every regard. It is our governor who troubles me. But my opinion is indirect." She looked at me quickly, then returned her eyes to the basket of fish, from which she plucked another and began scraping it. "Unlike yours, of course."

I continued working on the fish.

"Now, Emme, I already know you better than that. You do have an opinion here."

"Yes," I answered. "But I'm afraid you will not want to hear it."

"Why?"

"Because my thinking on it remains unfinished."

She laughed. "Oh, good," she said. "I believe I have just made a friend."

I smiled, too, keeping my eyes on my work. "As have I."

As the next several days passed, the meetings between John, Manteo, and Captain Stafford grew more frequent and urgent. Other assistants were sometimes included, as were John Wright and James Lasie, the two men who had been here before with Governor Lane. But whatever they discussed, they kept to themselves. None of the rest of us—at least, none of us women—had any notion that they were planning to attack Wanchese and his men before they could attack us. The result was nothing short of disastrous.

The attackers left our village at midnight a week after the parley on Croatoan. John, Manteo, Captain Stafford, and two dozen of our men boarded the pinnace and rowed it silently across the bay to Dasamonquepeuk. They arrived while it was still dark and, led by Manteo, they crept silently through the trees until they were on the mainland side of the village. From there they could see several Indians gathered around a fire, but not much else. At a command from John, our men rushed forward into the darkened village, some with swords and axes and others with their pistols and long harquebuses loaded and ready to fire. The astonished Indians all ran away, which was exactly what our men knew they would do, which is why they attacked from the inland side. Now the fleeing Indians had nowhere to go but into the reeds and marsh grasses along the shoreline.

For the ensuing hour, it was more a state of panicked confusion than a battle. The Englishmen followed the Indians into the reeds, but in the dark no one could very well see anyone else. Our men were fully dressed and most were wearing some sort of armor, either heavy metal corselets covering the upper body or lighter buff coats and chain mail, while the Indians were essentially naked. In the thick reeds, James Lasie, armed with a pistol, discharged it in the direction of the darkened silhouette of a bare torso and with an expiring grunt an Indian fell down dead. James shouted in triumph and began to reload. Meanwhile one of our other men aimed his harquebus at another fleeing naked back, but just before he fired, he saw that on the back was a baby. The Indian was a woman.

"Halloo, halloo!" he shouted at the top of his lungs. "There are women and children! Women and children! Beware your aim! Beware your aim!"

After that, the engagement became frenzied and disjointed, with both the English and the Indians calling to their own people from hidden locations in two different languages, all the while with Manteo rushing about trying to make sense of it. None of the men who later related it to us could match his own version with anyone else's, but most agreed that at some point after the sun rose and faces could be seen, one of the Indians ran toward Captain Stafford shouting, "Sta-for! Fren! Sta-for! Fren!" Stafford held the Indian at swordpoint and called for Manteo, who came running. Immediately he recognized the man. He was Cakisto, one of Manteo's cousins from Croatoan. Cakisto had recognized Captain Stafford from the parley.

In a great rush of words, Cakisto explained that all of the Indians there were from Manteo's village. As Cakisto related it, Wanchese and his people had fled immediately after killing George Howe, afraid of just this sort of retaliation from us. The Croatoans had learned of this just two days ago and a party of them had come over to take the food and other valuables that Wanchese's people had left behind in their rush to get away. The woman with the child who had barely escaped being shot was none other than the wife of one of the *wero-ances* of Croatoan.

Upon hearing this, Manteo flew into a great rage. He called together all of the Croatoans, brought them into the center of the village, sat them all down, and lectured them at length. This was their fault, he shouted. They should have known that Dasamonquepeuk was subject to English attack. They should have known that they were risking their lives in sneaking over here to steal Wanchese's crops. They should not have tried to steal the crops in the first place. They should have known that the English were in greater need of this food than were they, for the English had not arrived in Roanoke soon enough to plant their own. Most of all, they should not have come here at all without first getting his approval. They were all lucky, he thundered, that only one of them had been killed.

He then ordered them to gather all the crops and other things they came to steal and to place them all in the storage hold of the pinnace. Which is exactly what they did, the women and men together spending the rest of that day gathering in all of the ripe corn, pumpkins, squashes, and the broad leaves that the Indians called *uppowac*.

Meanwhile, John Wright, who had spent a lean winter here with the failed colony, suggested that they also dig up as many of the immature plants as they could fit into the pinnace so that we women could replant them here at Roanoke. It was a brilliant thought, for even though many of the seedlings that we were to replant in our gardens would not survive, just as many would. Their crops would keep us all from starving come winter.

Some of us would even learn to use the *uppowac* the way the Indians did, by burning it in clay pipes and inhaling the smoke. The Indians called it medicine, but it took no great schooling to recognize that its healing properties differed little—if at all—from those to be found in a flagon of strong ale, an insight that did little to restrain its intake by those of us who chose to try it. Relief from one's heavy cares is good relief indeed, am I not right? Only a flagellant would refuse it.

sixteen

For the next week after the botched attack on Dasamonquepeuk, there were frequent warm rain showers interspersed with periods of hot August sun. Such weather, uncomfortable as it made us all, especially poor Margery and Elenora in the very late stages of their pregnancies, was ideal for replanting the crops that Manteo and our men brought back in the pinnace. I threw myself wholeheartedly into the task, spending as many hours as I could tending to the gardens, not only my own but Margery's and Elenora's, as well, since the job was quite literally beyond their grasp. With the hot sun on my back and the cool, moist soil beneath me, I relished every minute of the time I spent on my knees with my bare hands in the ground, resettling the many dozens of plants in the three gardens.

In the cooler evenings, because the day had been so hot, many of us remained out of doors, gathered into small conversational groups around the community building in the center of our village. Not even the bothersome mosquitoes could drive us indoors, not until after the heat had dissipated from our cottages, making it possible to fall asleep. It was a wonderful opportunity to learn more about one another, and several seized the time to tell their own stories, some of them ringing with a clearer clang of truth than others. Audry and I generally sat together, commenting in whispered asides to each other in response to some of the more obvious embellishments. Our favorite was John Spendlove, who introduced himself as a gentleman and proceeded, in the telling of his various comical anecdotes, to prove that he was anything but. Others were more serious, but most tended to end their short histories with a positive statement about how much he or she was looking forward to growing our small colony here in the new world. All said, although it didn't last nearly long enough, that warm August week, with its days of planting and evenings of camaraderie, was the best of time for us as a colony.

As for John and me, I cannot say the same was true. Our estrangement continued. We went about our daily tasks separately, ate meals communally with other colonists, and slept separately in the upstairs chamber of the house. I do not say here that it was his house, for I considered it to be ours equally, even though we were not yet married and he had not yet made our betrothal public. I still fully expected that we would marry. John had asked me and I had accepted. The timing was his to choose, not mine, and I could wait. If the lack of that announcement meant that I remained nothing more than a housekeeper in the minds of the others, it bothered me not at all. In the still-developing social structure of the colony, there was little distance between the lowliest and the governor himself.

At the end of that week, John White called the entire colony together for a ceremony that, though few of us realized it at the time, would throw that social structure into permanent disarray. Unfortunately, I was one of the few who knew in advance that there would be trouble.

The night before, after the evening's sharing of tales by the community building, I bade Audry good night and walked home. I came through the front door to see a gathering of men seated around our dining table, deep in discussion. The room was lit by lanterns and extra candles, and when I appeared all the men came quickly to their feet, shuffling their chairs and pushing small movements of air that blew against the unprotected candles and sent shimmering shadows and light dancing throughout the room.

"Mrs. Merrimoth," they all murmured together in greeting.

"Gentlemen," I answered. "Please forgive me. I was unaware of any meeting this evening."

"It was unscheduled," said John. "The fault is not yours."

John's voice was strained and I could see from his florid complexion that he had been arguing. The same tightness appeared on the faces of the others, all of them assistants: Ananias Dare, Dyonis Harvey, Roger Bailey, Christopher Cooper, Thomas Stevens, John Nichols, William Fullwood, James Plat, Roger Prat, John Sampson, Humphrey Dimmocke, and, as I just now realized with a start, Simon Fernandez. In the dim light, I had not initially noticed him.

All I could do was stare. What was this? As far as I knew, it was the first time Simon had come ashore from the *Lyon*. Not only that—this wasn't just an informal gathering of assistants, it was a full meeting of them all.

"Shall I produce beverages and sweets, sir?" I asked John. The table was empty.

"No, thank you, Em—"

"A fine idea, Mrs. Merrimoth," interrupted Simon. "A bit of cooling off might boot us all well at the moment. And I for one would be more than grateful for anything sweet you might be willing to share with a hungry sailor."

Several of the others nodded, and John irritably waved his approval. I ignored the knowing smirk that remained on Simon's face as I repaired to the pantry. The men continued their urgent discussion in lowered voices. But our house was small and there was no door to the pantry. As I prepared decanters of sack and ale and cut a fruitcake into small pieces, I could hear them plainly.

They were talking about Manteo. From what I could gather, as part of the new colony's charter, Sir Walter Raleigh had commanded that in return for his faithful services to the English, Manteo was to be christened into the church and be named lord of the surrounding lands encompassing Roanoke and part of the nearby mainland, including Dasamonquepeuk. But that appointment was predicated on the idea that Manteo would be left here to govern this portion of Raleigh's new world holdings while the colony sailed north to be set up in Chesepiok, where John would be governor. Now that the colony had been set up at Roanoke instead, John and some of his supporters wanted to rescind Raleigh's order.

"I will not share my governorship with an un-Christian savage!" said John, raising his voice.

"Nor should he!" agreed Christopher Cooper, John's most ardent supporter. An overweight and humorless man with small eyes and a fixed scowl, he had been a magistrate or a clerk of some sort back in England. He never seemed to have a thought of his own but could be counted on to parrot every word of John's. I found him odious.

"You have no choice," countered Simon. "Raleigh's order carries the weight of law here. And furthermore, as we have repeatedly said here tonight, Manteo is to be christened. That portion of your objection will be moot, sir."

"Bah! I simply will not have it!"

"Bah yourself, sir!" retorted Simon. "You simply will have it."

I came back into the room and set the drinks and cakes on the table. Simon reached for a goblet and a piece of cake, then leaned back in his chair.

"Tell us, Mrs. Merrimoth," he said as he popped the cake into his mouth. "A fresh set of ears. What are your thoughts on the matter?"

"On which matter, sir?"

"Hah!" he laughed, sending small crumbs spewing from his mouth. The others laughed, too. All but John and, of course, Christopher Cooper, who glanced at John for his cue and then matched his master's scowl.

"Indeed, Mrs. Merrimoth," said Ananias. "Of course you have been listening. I for one know you to be a woman of parts. What say you?"

The others nodded, most of them still smiling. It was clear that all but John and Christopher Cooper were glad to have a bit of light respite from their contentions. Who was I to deny them? This was an arena in which I had played before, a room full of men with drinks in their hands, all looking at me.

"What I say to that, good sir, is that the parts of this woman normally concern themselves with activities other than politics."

"Hear, hear!" shouted Ananias amidst the general laughter. He raised his goblet. "To the parts of Mrs. Merrimoth!"

"To the parts of Mrs. Merrimoth!" responded most of the others.

"Enough!" shouted John. He came to his feet, livid with anger. "We are discussing a most serious matter here! Those who wish to explore my housekeeper's parts shall arrange for that lewdness on their own time, and certainly not here in the governor's household." He turned to me, as angry and frightened as I had ever seen him. "As for you, Mrs. Merrimoth, you are excused!"

Like they had on the trail from the Croatoan village, his words struck me physically. The others all went silent. I turned and started toward the door, working to hold back my tears. But in the smoldering week that had passed between us, my feelings for John had cooled considerably, and my ability to stand my ground before his insults had strengthened. Tears did not come to my eyes. Halfway to the door, I stopped, then turned to face the silent room of men.

"You asked for my thoughts," I said. "So you shall have them. I have no standing here. You all must decide the question. But if Manteo is not granted that which is due to him, if John White remains our sole governor here, I shall not stay. I shall return to England aboard the *Lyon* and I shall encourage as many of the others as I can to do the same."

I faced John directly. "I, for one, gentlemen, shall not allow my future to be in the hands of one whose ego supplants his reason at every opportunity, and who seems so inadequate to the task of governance. Not even God can save us from one such as that. Good night to you all."

I turned to leave.

"Mrs. Merrimoth!" shouted John.

I kept walking.

"You are free to go nowhere, Mrs. Merrimoth! Neither you nor any other colonist will ever leave this colony. You are all indentured to me!"

That I could not leave unanswered. I stopped. "Master Harvey," I said without turning around. "When I agreed to come here with you and Mrs. Harvey, was I indentured?"

"No," said Dyonis. "You were not. No one among us is indentured except by private contract among themselves."

"Master Fernandez," I added. "If I were to request passage back to England, would you grant it to me?"

"Without hesitation and with great pleasure," he answered. I knew he was smiling at John.

"And if others were to join me, would you offer them passage, as well?"

"I would indeed, madam."

"Good night, then," I said. And I left.

I spent that night in Audry's cottage and remained there for the next ten days. Although I did not know it then, I had spent my last night under the same roof as John White.

At noon the next day, we gathered in the community building, most of the others buzzing with questions as to why they had been called away from their work. I certainly knew more than they did, and wondered: Was Manteo to be christened and elevated to governor or not?

My answer came as soon as I saw John and Manteo entering the building, accompanied by Manteo's mother and several of the Croatoan *weroances,* all of them standing a full head above even the tallest of our men. They were followed by all of the assistants, save Simon, who, I surmised, had returned to the *Lyon.* At that point, I knew that John had lost the argument and had either been forced or persuaded to follow Raleigh's order. John had put on his finest clothing and was wearing his ceremonial sword. Manteo was cloaked in the most elegant of native deerskin robes, dyed a rich green and fringed with hundreds of shining pearls. On his head was a crown of shining metal, not very different from the one his mother wore. When all were aligned at the center of the building, John asked for silence and proceeded to explain—at great length, of course, and taking the credit for himself—what we were about to witness.

The ceremony itself took less time than John's introduction to it. Since there was not a clergyman among us, John performed the brief christening ceremony himself, reading the familiar text from the Book of Common Prayer. Then, in an equally short ceremony, John read from a scroll and formally appointed Manteo Lord of Roanoke and Dasamonquepeuk. As always, Manteo showed no emotion. Puzzlement and perplexity were the two most common expressions I saw among the others. In less than an hour, Manteo and his fellows had left in their canoes to return to Croatoan and we colonists were all back at work.

For the time being, we now had two governors.

seventeen

The week that followed Manteo's appointment was even more hectic than those that preceded it, and those had been anything but lax. The last of our colony's supplies and foodstuffs were finally transferred from the *Lyon* and the flyboat to land. This meant that Simon and his sailors were able to begin refitting the ships for their journey back across the ocean to England. Between our own efforts to finish our village and the comings and goings of the sailors as they cut wood and hauled fresh water to the two ships, the colony was as busy as a disrupted anthill.

In the midst of this activity, Elenora Dare went into labor, and, on the eighteenth of August, delivered a healthy little girl. We all rejoiced at this good omen. Because the baby was the first English child born in Virginia, Ananias and Elenora gave that as her name: Virginia Dare. Quite a lovely name, I thought, and one that pleased even John White, bringing him out of his vile mood for several days. The following Sunday, Virginia was christened by John in a ceremony attended by all. Manteo and his mother, Benginoor, came to pay their respects, and although Manteo and John conversed politely at the midday feast that followed the service, it was plain to me that their outward conviviality was a veneer maintained by them both. I had no doubt that a confrontation was bound to occur.

Here I must pause again in the writing of this journal to consider the nature of my own memory. As I write this, alone in my hut preparing for tomorrow's council meeting, I work from nothing but my recollections, which seem perfectly accurate to me. But as I pondered earlier, how can I be sure? I have just written that I had no doubt that a confrontation between Manteo and John was to occur, but that memory is now colored by the fact that the confrontation truly did occur shortly thereafter. Do I now give myself false credit for being clairvoyant? Did I really see the confrontation coming before it did?

No matter. I can only write the truth as it appears to me now—and it appears to me now that I surely did foresee the confrontation.

The trouble came unexpectedly, borne quite literally on the wind that began to rise the day after Virginia Dare's christening. At first, none of us saw the new weather as anything unusual, but during the night, it turned much worse. Limbs cracked in the trees outside our compound's palisade, and the wind moaned throughout the night as the storm rose. Morning came, late and dark, and with it came sheets of rain driven sideways by the gale. There was nothing to do but stay indoors, though some of the men hurried to the shoreline to set out an extra anchor on the pinnace and haul our small boats up the beach as the wind-driven tide rose higher and higher. Eventually they had to drag the boats all the way onto high ground and lash them to trees as the beach went completely underwater. As to the pinnace, all they could do was pray for its two anchors to hold. Already the wind was blowing the tops off the waves even here in the protected sound.

Inside the cottage I shared with Audry and Thomas, the increasing wind found every opening, gusting enough even indoors to occasionally blow out candles. It was frightening, as strong as any sudden thunderstorm back home, but lasting for hours instead of minutes and growing steadily stronger. As the three of us sat in the center of the main room, listening as trees broke in the forest outside the palisade, it suddenly occurred to me that it had to be even worse out on the water, where Simon and his two ships lay at anchor.

"What will happen to the *Lyon* and the flyboat?" I asked Thomas.

"They will have left already," said Thomas. "Their safety lies in the open ocean, where they cannot be driven ashore by the tempest."

"But aren't many of the crew still here?" asked Audry. "Working on the resupply of the vessels?"

"True enough." Thomas nodded. "That will make for some long watches by those still aboard."

When the storm finally abated after two days and we all reemerged to assess the damage, among those wandering about were the stranded sailors. Until their ships returned, they pitched in with the rest of us in the general cleaning up of the village.

The first order of business was to straighten and relash the part of our palisade that had blown down in the wind. Since the palisade was built from heavy pine tree trunks that had been felled and hauled to the site, it was a job that could only be done by the strongest of our men, including the stranded sailors, who were used to working with heavy timbers, strong ropes, and sturdy knots. Audry and I, along with several other women, went outside the palisade to watch as the work progressed, since there were few of our normal chores that could be done. Our gardens were still under several inches of rainwater and we'd have to wait to get back to work until most of it had drained away. The inland sound was so stirred up that no fish or crabs would be caught for several days, at least. And after having been trapped under roofs day and night throughout the storm, certainly none of us wanted to stay inside doing housework.

From the outside, our collection of cottages and utility buildings no longer looked like a village. It looked very much like the fort that it had been. The palisade itself was a dark wall of vertical tree trunks lashed tightly together, twenty feet tall and surrounding the entire village. The entrance wasn't a gate. Instead, the two walls there did not meet, but passed each other for a span of ten or twenty feet, overlapping so that in order to enter the village, one had to pass between the two overlapping sections for several long strides. Atop the palisade here—and at other strategic overlooks—was a guard tower from which our defenders could easily shoot down at any enemy that tried to enter. Now, after the storm, some of our men were doing repairs up in the guard towers, for each tower had been largely exposed to the fearful winds.

Just outside the entrance, several of our men were working with knives and hatchets to free a tangle of old line from a portion of the original section that had blown down in the storm. Four or five of the tall pine trunks now lay jumbled upon the soaking, muddy ground, and the ropes that had tied them together were hopelessly intertwined. It was messy, difficult work, and most were so splattered with mud, pine chips, and frayed bits of hemp from the ropes at which they sawed and hacked that it was hard to tell one man from another. Although I didn't spot him right away, among the men working on the palisade was Codman, the frightened sailor who had told Simon and John and me about Darby Glane's real purpose in jumping ship and running off to find the Spanish.

While Audry and I watched the workers, John and several of the assistants came out to inspect the progress of the repair, tipping their hats to us ladies as they did. That must have attracted Codman's attention, for he looked up from his work. He and I then recognized each other, and he, too, touched his hat, knife in hand. It would have been better for the poor man had he been less polite, for when he did that, he drew John's attention, as well.

"You there!" commanded John when he spied Codman. "Come here!"

Then, as soon as the fearful little sailor approached the governor and his fellows, John cried, "Seize him! He is a traitor!"

Codman tried to run, but the men with John quickly overtook and caught him. They brought him before John, who then spoke directly to him.

"You may have fooled your ship's master with your lies, but not me!" John said. "Had I known you were here and not at sea with him, I'd have ordered you arrested. Your treasonous tale has cost this colony its proper home and now you shall pay for it!"

"But, sar," cried Codman, "I told no—"

"Silence! " interrupted John. Then to the others he ordered, "Take him to the guardhouse and clap him in bilboes! He shall be hanged as soon as I write his indictment!"

"Hanged?" shouted several of the sailors. They rushed toward John and the assistants, who quickly drew their swords and pistols, forcing the sailors to stop. But the distraction gave Codman a chance to try once again to run. He wrested himself free of the grip of William Fullwood and started to rush away. He still had his knife in his hand and in his panic he ran right toward me.

"Mum!" he cried. "Help me!"

"Halt there!" shouted John. I glanced to see that he now had a pistol in his hand, pointed at Codman as he ran toward me.

The terrified sailor was now almost upon me. "Tell them it isn't true, mum!" he cried. "Help me—"

Boom!

With a loud clap and a shower of sparks and smoke, the pistol went off just as Codman reached me. The bullet struck his back with an audible *whap!* and knocked him to his knees right before me. He dropped the knife, stared up at me, and tried to say one more thing; then he threw his arms around my waist, coughed blood, and collapsed dead at my feet.

I don't know that I screamed. Audry and the other women most certainly did, long and loud and shrill. That and the gunshot itself brought the entire colony rushing out. For several minutes, all was confusion. In the center of it I stood, staring back and forth at poor Codman on the ground, at the red stains of his blood on my dress, and at the others all around me, some shouting questions, others simply staring in disbelief at the unfathomable tableau so suddenly and grotesquely laid out before them. Why I did not faint dead away I cannot explain, but I did not.

It was Audry who came to my aid. Putting her arm around my waist and gesturing at the others to clear a path, she ushered me back into the village, waving off the questions as she did.

"Ask your governor!" she shouted irritably to those who stood in our way. "Ask your governor! This woman needs assistance and fresh clothing. Make way! Ask your governor!"

And ask him they did, closing behind us *en masse* as Audry hustled me back to her cottage where, in a daze, I shed my dress and handed it to her. In her fireplace, the embers of the previous night's fire still glowed. Audry balled up my blood-soaked dress and threw it onto the coals, where, with a bit of prodding, it eventually burst into flame.

"Oh, Audry," I said. "Why did you do that? It could have been washed."

"Yes, Emme," she said, and nodded. "The blood could have been washed away, but not the memory. Am I not right?"

"But I have so few dresses."

"I will make you another. That's a promise."

With that, I broke down and cried.

eighteen

The killing of Codman consumed the colony. For the rest of that day and far into the night, people gathered in groups, demanding to know what had happened. John said nothing. Hounded by their questions, he repaired to his house with his five supporters among the assistants: Christopher Cooper, William Fullwood, John Nichols, James Plat, and Humphrey Dimmocke. Undeterred, the rest of the assistants—Ananias, Dyonis, John Sampson, Roger Prat, Roger Bailey, and Thomas Stevens joined with regular colonists and the sailors from the *Lyon* outside John's house, demanding that he come out and explain himself. After dark, they remained there, carrying lit torches. It began to look like a witch hunt.

Eventually, Ananias took charge. He called for a council, though it was not his prerogative to do so. No one but the governor had ever called one. But Ananias asked for a vote among the assistants to call one anyway. Since five of the eleven assistants stood with him with torches in their hands, the outcome was certain. A council was called immediately, as everyone had already gathered there, and no one wished to go home, only to reconvene in the morning.

When Audry came back to her cottage to tell me this news, I told her I did not want to attend the council. The memory of Codman's pleading eyes as he collapsed against me and died had kept me awake in a constant nightmare ever since. All I wanted was to make the image go away. As the others gathered, I asked Audry to leave me in her house and to tell anyone who asked that I was indisposed and could not attend. It certainly was true enough, though apparently not good enough. Not long after the council had convened, Audry came back to get me.

"You must come," she said. "The assistants have called for you."

The community building was filled to overflowing. So many torches and candles had been lit that smoke was coming out through the open doors and windows. Every colonist and stranded sailor was there, packed together in the dim and flickering orange firelight. In the open center, John stood at one end, backed by his cadre of five assistants. At the other end stood Ananias and the rest of the assistants. Audry led me through the shoulder-to-shoulder onlookers to the center. As people began to notice I was there, the babble of voices died away. By the time Audry and I reached the center, all had gone quiet.

"You asked for her," she said to Ananias. "Here she is."

"Thank you for coming, Mrs. Merrimoth," he said. "We all understand how upsetting today's events must have been for you. But there are questions raised here for which you may have some answers. We would like to hear those answers."

I nodded.

"First, did you know this man Codman before today?"

I nodded, drawing a murmur from the crowd.

"Where did you know him?"

"Aboard the *Lyon*," I answered softly.

"And how did you make his acquaintance?"

"I did not actually make his acquaintance, sir. We were never introduced."

"Then how did you know him?"

"He came into Master Fernandez's quarters to make a report. I was there, along with the governor."

"And what was his report?"

I looked at John. He was impassive, staring straight ahead, refusing to meet my eyes. In the odd light, his eyes gleamed, tinged with fire.

"Answer the question, Mrs. Merrimoth."

I kept looking at John, awaiting a signal, a nod or a shake of his head. Anything. He did not move, did not acknowledge my entreaty. Dearly I wished that Simon were here, but of course he was not. The *Lyon* and the flyboat, if they had survived the storm, were still far out at sea. I took a deep breath to calm myself. "I do not think I am at liberty to say, sir. With all respect."

"And why are you not at liberty to say?"

"Because his report was to the master of the *Lyon* and the governor of the colony, sir, not to me. I am just a common colonist who happened to overhear it. Surely it is not my place to divulge the contents of a sailor's report to his master. Surely that right belongs to the master and to the governor, not to me. Am I wrong, sir?"

The room broke into many voices, each trying to be heard. Ananias and the assistants on his side urgently conversed among themselves. At his end, John finally looked at me, just long enough to nod his head. It took Ananias and the assistants several minutes to restore order.

"Governor White," said Ananias, as the crowd quieted, "will you tell us what Codman had to say in the report just described by Mrs. Merrimoth?"

"I will not, sir."

"Why will you not, sir?"

"Because the report he made was deliberately false, designed only to incite unwarranted fear among this colony, and therefore traitorous. I will not carry out his dirty work by repeating the false rumor he tried to spread. What matters is that the man was a traitor and deserved to be hanged, a fate which he escaped only by virtue of his attempted violent attack on Mrs. Merrimoth, which was thwarted by me. We are well rid of him. He deserved to die."

Ananias and his assistants again urgently conferred and the voices rose once more. Once Ananias finished with his discussion and quelled the voices of everyone else, he turned back to me.

"Mrs. Merrimoth, I and the other assistants standing here constitute a majority. We have agreed that, because our governor has refused to tell us what Codman said in his report, you are now free—nay, required—to tell us all what the man had to say. Please do so now."

I tried one more time for a signal from John. He did not look my way, but simply shook his head. Behind me, Audry whispered, "You must answer."

She was right. John was wrong. I turned back to Ananias. "He said he was with Darby Glane when Darby ran away on the island."

"What else did he report?"

"I hesitate to say, sir."

"Why?"

"Because I cannot recall it with precision, sir. I fear that I will misrepresent him."

From behind, I felt Audry's hand on my back. "Well said," she whispered in my ear.

Ananias was unmoved. "We can take that into consideration, Mrs. Merrimoth. Please continue."

I looked at Audry behind me. She shrugged, then nodded. There was nothing for it but to tell the tale.

"As best I remember," I said, "Codman's story was that Darby had confided to him that he had been paid in advance, back in England, to jump ship as soon as we got to Spanish territory. He, Darby, was then to find the Spanish and tell them that we had arrived in the new world to establish a colony."

"Liar!"

The shout came from a female voice across the room. It was Elizabeth Glane, who pushed her way to the front so she could face me across the center opening.

"Liar! Me Darby ne'er wont say such a thing! Never!" Her wide face was flushed, almost matching her unkempt red hair. "She lies, your honor! She lies! Me Darby's a good man!"

"Please restrain yourself, Mrs. Glane," said Ananias. "If you wish to speak later, you must hold your tongue now!"

"I won't hold it, sar! Not against her—she is a liar! Nay, sar, she is a witch! A witch putting false tales into the mouth of me dear, God-fearin' husband!"

The room erupted. An accusation of witchcraft was serious, and everyone knew it. We all knew of the trials in Chelmsford, and though I had not gone, many of the assembled had attended the trials—and the subsequent hangings.

"Silence!" shouted Ananias. "Silence, everyone!" The room quieted, and he was able to continue. "Mrs. Glane, that is a most serious accusation. If it slipped from your tongue in anger, we will understand. But you must retract it if that is the case. What say you?"

Elizabeth glared at me, her stout frame tense and shaking and her visage alive with hatred, the likes of which I had never seen. "I will *not*!"

I barely heard the voices rising around me. Was I now to be tried as a witch? There was no good outcome from that. Just how many of my fellow colonists believed in witchery, I knew not. But if enough did, my fate was sealed. Acquittals in the Chelmsford trials had been few. Public hanging had been the usual outcome.

"Say something, Emme," urged Audry behind me. "Say something now, before this progresses!"

I knew I had to. I stepped forward. "Sir," I said to Ananias, and the room quieted once more. "I asked not to relate Codman's story, but you required it anyway. I said that I feared I would misstate it, but you required me to relate it nonetheless."

My voice was shaking. I forced myself to continue. "And now, because I have assented to your order and related a sailor's report which was not mine to repeat, because I have told this assembly the same story that both John White and Simon Fernandez would tell were you to subject them to the same order, I am to be accused of witchcraft? That is not right, sir, as everyone here must assuredly know."

Some of the assembled colonists seemed to agree with me, others with Elizabeth. Someone said, "Let us hear the governor!"

Ananias bowed his head. For a few seconds, he considered, and then he faced John.

"Sir," he said, "Mrs. Merrimoth's defense against Mrs. Glane's accusation is that you would tell the same story if ordered to do so. Is that not the case, Mrs. Merrimoth?"

"It is, sir," I answered. "We both heard it at the same time."

"Then, sir," continued Ananias to John, "it comes down to you. You are our governor. I cannot give you an order. I can only request that, in the name of the truth we all seek here, you break your self-imposed silence on the matter. A life may hang in the balance."

I do not know how long it took John to decide. The passage of time was wholly absent from my awareness of what was happening.

"Under the circumstances I have no choice," he said eventually. The room went completely still as John stepped forward. This time, he faced me directly.

"Mrs. Merrimoth is well known to me. She has many faults. She certainly is no exemplar of modesty or virtue. Nor, as she has just demonstrated, does she have the good sense to know when it is her place to remain dutifully silent. But she is not a witch. She is telling the truth. Her version of Codman's story does not differ from the one I would tell."

That produced the loudest uproar yet. Elizabeth Glane's cries of outrage were completely drowned out in the general outburst. It took Ananias a very long time to regain control of the meeting. When he had, he kept his attention on John.

"Have you anything to add, sir?"

"I do not, sir. I spoke only in defense of Mrs. Merrimoth against the false accusation of Mrs. Glane. I have already said that Codman's story was a traitorous lie, one that should not have been granted the dignity of a public airing, which I tried to prevent. All I wished to convey here was that Mrs. Merrimoth is party neither to the man's dishonesty nor to his treason. She merely repeated what Codman said. She is guilty of insubordination, not dishonesty. And certainly not witchcraft."

The murmur that spread through the crowd was one of agreement and assent.

Ananias raised his hands. "The accusation against Mrs. Merrimoth is dismissed," he announced. "Her version of Codman's tale we will now accept as fact, since it is corroborated by our governor. It is late. This council is now ended. We shall reconvene in the morning to discuss the implications of the story we have now been told."

"The falsehood, you mean, sir," said John.

"Perhaps it is, sir, and perhaps it is not. Either way, there are implications that we all must consider. Let us now all repair to our beds and give some thought to the morrow's deliberations. Good night."

People began to disperse, still speaking among themselves. Elizabeth Glane was not assuaged, but she knew when to retreat, and she did so, quietly slipping out of the community building, leaving me with one more baleful look as she turned to go. All I could do in return was feel sorry for her. She had only tried to defend her husband and, as a result, her status in the colony was now effectively destroyed. A false accusation of witchcraft was the same as an attempted murder. What could she now do? Where could she now go? And how could she and I coexist in this small community?

"Come, Emme," said Audry. "Let us try to find you a bit of the sleep you need."

"A futile search," I answered.

"Let us embark on it anyway."

nineteen

The day after our late-night council was sultry and hot even in its early hours. The motionless air weighed oppressively upon us all as we gathered in the community building, putting most in a perspiring bad humor before Ananias had even called the council to order. At least we had a roof to shade us from the August sun as it rose higher and hotter through the morning. No one could have stood for those hours in its direct heat.

When Audry and I arrived, I was taken aback to see Manteo there along with several of his *weroances*. Later I was to learn that word of Codman's death had somehow gotten swiftly to the village at Croatoan and that Manteo and his senior men had paddled all night to get here.

Ananias did not stand on ceremony. Right away, he stated the council's purpose: to assess the tale told by Codman. "The question is plain," he said, "and it comes in two parts. First, how much credence to place on the story itself—was Codman telling the truth about Darby

Glane's intention to alert the Spanish, or was he lying? Second, if we conclude that there is a possibility that the Spanish have indeed been alerted to our existence, what are we to do about it?"

There followed a lengthy and impassioned debate. By my count, the colony seemed evenly split between those who believed Codman and those who did not. John was vehemently in the latter camp, of course, as was Elizabeth Glane.

I tried not to speak, but eventually was called on to do so. When it came to his turn to express an opinion, Thomas Hewet, the lawyer, asked me instead:

"Mrs. Merrimoth, of all of us here, only you and the governor were there when Codman made his report to Simon Fernandez. The governor characterizes what he heard as a traitorous lie. How do you characterize what you heard? Did Codman seem to be telling the truth or not?"

I had expected the question, though from whom and in what form, I had no idea. After the night council, I had not gone directly to bed, but had instead stayed up for more than an hour, discussing with Audry what I should say this morning when asked. The problem was that John had come to my aid against Elizabeth's accusation, had possibly even saved my life. Was I now to repay that unexpected act by doing the opposite to him? But, as Audry pointed out, it wasn't John to whom I owed my answer. It was Codman.

"Had he not begged you with his dying eyes to save him?" she'd asked. "To bear witness and exonerate him before these very same people? And is this not the time and place to grant the poor man his dying plea?"

It was, I had to agree. Thus my answer was ready, much as I did not want to give it.

"He seemed to me, sir, to be telling the truth," I said.

I had expected an uproar in response, but the room, instead, grew even quieter. Every eye turned toward John. For a moment, he was silent, and then he stepped forward.

"I said last night that Mrs. Merrimoth is not a witch," he said. "She is not. She is a woman, nothing more. Her opinion is, like that of most women, subject to the wind and just as variable. Ask her tomorrow, nay, ask her in an hour, and she may tell a wholly different tale. Pay her no mind. Listen instead to your governor."

Some of the men laughed, but not many. Others hissed and booed.

"My tale in this matter will never vary," I insisted. "But if the honest witness of a simple woman be not good enough for this council, sir, then I pray you to inform it of the heated discussion between you and Master Fernandez that took place immediately after Codman's report."

"I do not recall the particulars of such a discussion, Mrs. Merrimoth."

"Then apparently the wind blows more erratically through your mind than it does through that of a mere woman, sir. For I recall it with precision."

That did produce an uproar, mostly of laughter directed at John. He did not take it well. "Enough!" he shouted. "I will not be insulted like this! This council is now disbanded! Colonists, your governor commands you to return to your work!"

No one did, of course. Everyone stood, either shocked, perplexed, or with looks of pity. And a growing number appeared angry. Ananias quieted them, and then turned to me.

"Please enlighten us, Mrs. Merrimoth."

I did so, while John glowered at me from the far end of the room. I left nothing that I could recall from my narrative, relating Simon's stubborn insistence that the colony would be in too much danger if it were planted, as planned, at Chesepiok; John's equally adamant position that the colony must go there anyway, since it was Raleigh's order to do so; and Simon's refusal to endanger the colony by carrying us there.

"And so they remained completely at odds," I concluded. "The stalemate was resolved by Master Fernandez, when he ordered his sailors to leave the governor and his initial party ashore here at Roanoke, and to then convey the rest of us ashore. That, sir, is why we are here and not at Chesepiok. Because Master Fernandez did indeed believe Codman's story."

Ananias turned to John. "Sir, is this true? Are we here now because Simon Fernandez decided it and not you?"

John did not answer right away. How could he? To admit the truth was the end of his authority. While he hesitated, one of the stranded sailors stepped forward.

"Sars," he said, "my name is Ezekiah Compit. I can attest to part of it, I can. Me mates will back me on it, sars, if ye will 'ave me testimony." The other sailors murmured their assent.

"By all means, Compit. What say you?"

"Sars, we was ordered by the ship's master to do as the lady says. We was told to put the guv'nor and his men ashore and not to bring 'em back, no matter what the guv'nor ordered. Master Fernandez told us to ignore the guv'nor's orders and obey only his. Which is what we done, sars."

That was the end of John's governorship. A great cry of outrage went up from the assemblage. By the time Ananias regained control of the meeting, John and his cadre had been hooted out of the community building and driven into his house.

At that point, Manteo, who had stood immobile, flanked by his *weroances,* throughout the proceeding, stepped forward and raised his arm. The voices soon quieted.

"My friends," he said, in his singsong English, "regardless of why you are here, you are all welcome. You are all my friends, and I will be a good governor to you, as I have sworn to be. I and my people will protect you from Wanchese and his people. We will provide whatever guidance you need as you establish your town here."

Most everyone seemed very happy to hear that. If any held reservations to being governed solely by Manteo, none voiced them. Only he and his people, after all, could offer us the protection and guidance he had just promised.

Manteo continued. "Ananias Dare has been the principal assistant. Henceforth, I will recognize him as your leader. Good day to you all." With that pronouncement, Manteo and his *weroances* took their leave.

The rest of us followed, though slowly. Many wanted to continue the discussion, but others had had enough. There really was work to be done, not least in importance the repair of the palisade, which had been interrupted by the shooting. Ananias seemed to sense that the mood of the majority favored ending the council, and so he did just that.

As Audry and I walked back toward her house, she surprised me by expressing approval of Ananias. "He seems adequate to the job," she said. "I thought his handling of the situation was more than competent. And as father of our community's firstborn child, I can only assume the long-term health of the colony is his primary concern. We may finally be in good hands."

"I think you are right," I said. What I kept to myself was how much I, too, had found myself looking upon him with new eyes, a view that I knew from much experience I would do well to keep exactly there: entirely to myself.

twenty

The oppressive August heat continued. Even late at night, it was difficult to sleep. And in the middle of this inauspicious weather, Margery went into labor.

By that time, the Harveys and I had mended our fences, at least well enough for me to be invited back as wet nurse for their newborn. In truth, they had nowhere else to turn. No other woman in the colony was in position to take on the new baby and not only was I available, but I was just as enthusiastic as I had been from the beginning. I could barely wait to get my hands on the child.

Margery's labor was long, not unexpected for her first, but she did not tolerate it well. Beginning around midnight, she suffered terribly—and quite vocally—and it continued for nearly twenty-four hours before she finally delivered a healthy baby boy. By that time, Audry, I, and several other women had been attending to Margery around the clock. After the delivery, nothing seemed out of the ordinary. She did not bleed excessively, the afterbirth came naturally, and she was alert and wanting to hold her new son. She and Dyonis named him Valentyne.

Afterward, the other women were free to return to their own chores, but I had to spend much of my time with Margery. I had to get my own milk flowing as soon as possible, so whenever the infant woke and began to cry for another feeding, I had to be there to let the hungry little thing try to get what he craved. Then I would hand Valentyne to Margery for a real feeding. It was not the first time I had wet-nursed, so I knew this would go on for a week or more before I could produce enough flow to take over the feeding on my own.

For the first two days, all went according to plan. All three of us—Margery, Valentyne, and I—were settling into the routine and getting along well. But sometime during the night before the third day, Margery took a fever. By that morning, she was burning up and delirious, and by midafternoon, it was obvious to all of us who had tried to care for her that she was not going to recover. She died just after sunset.

We were all stunned by the suddenness of it, but none more so than Dyonis. He was completely undone. No one could approach him, not even Ananias, his oldest and dearest friend in the colony, and not even I, with his newborn son in my arms. He withdrew completely into himself, and all we could see to do was to let him be, hoping that the passing of time would alleviate his suffering.

Meanwhile, I had a more immediate problem. My milk had not started and now I had a hungry baby to feed. Luckily, Elenora was now in full flow from nursing her own little Virginia, and she agreed without hesitation. The extra burden would only be for a week or two, until I could relieve her of it.

It would have been far easier to move the baby to Elenora's cottage, but that was something I could not do without Dyonis's permission, and he remained in his unapproachable trance, speaking to no one. So for two days, I shuttled between the Harvey cottage and the Dare cottage, carrying Valentyne back and forth at all hours of the day and night to let him first suckle at my breast and then drink his fill from Elenora. It soon became untenable.

"What if we have another storm?" asked Audry. "You can't be carrying an infant outside in something like that."

The next time I carried Valentyne to the Dares' house, Audry came with me. Together we asked Ananias to use his authority to allow me to move into his house with Valentyne for as long as his wife, Elenora, was still nursing both babies.

"How long will that be?" he asked.

"Until Mrs. Merrimoth's own milk comes in," answered Audry. "Perhaps a week."

"Why do you not just leave the baby here until then?"

Audry glanced at me, then back to Ananias. "Sir, do I take it that you are not aware of certain aspects of this process?"

Ananias looked perplexed.

Audry seemed perturbed. "Sir, in order for Mrs. Merrimoth to produce milk, she must . . . give suck to the baby. This gives rise to her own production of milk."

"I see," he said, looking uncomfortably back and forth between Audry and me. "I had no idea."

"May she move into your house, sir?" Audry replied. "It will be better for all concerned."

"Yes, yes, of course," he said, recovering his composure. "By all means. Far be it from me to stand in the way of stimulating the admirable breasts of Mrs. Merrimoth. In fact, I would be pleased to offer my assistance."

"This is hardly the time for levity, sir," Audry admonished him.

He folded his hands and bowed. "Of course, Mrs. Tappan. Please forgive me."

As we walked back to Dyonis's house to pack up for my move, Audry shook her head. "Can you imagine?" she scoffed. "How puerile. And from our newly appointed leader."

"I thought it was funny," I admitted. Audry looked sharply at me, so I added quickly, "In its puerile way, of course."

95

"Hopeless," Audry said. "Utterly hopeless."

That day Audry and I moved the baby and me into Ananias and Elenora's cottage. It was not as large as the governor's house, but it was one of the few single-family dwellings in the colony, befitting Ananias's initial standing as principal assistant. There was no second floor, just a low-ceilinged storage area. The first floor was divided into just two rooms, the bedroom where they and the baby slept and a larger room that held a dining table, several straight-backed chairs, various cupboards and chests, Elenora's spinning wheel and loom, and a fireplace. Out the back door were a roofed kitchen hut, drying yard, and small garden. Audry and I carried Valentyne's cot from Dyonis's house to the main room of the Dares', and then she and I did the same from her house with the narrow day bed upon which I had been sleeping.

It looked like a workable arrangement. I could even tend to Elenora's garden for her and do the cooking. My only regret was that I would now have to sleep in my heavy cotton shift rather than in the nude, the way I—and most of the others, I assumed—did in this heat wave. But with Ananias under the same roof, I knew better than to provoke him. His earlier offer of "assistance" had been delivered only partly in jest, as his eyes had made plain to me. There had been nothing puerile in his gaze.

twenty-one

The day after I and the baby moved in with the Dare family, we were all awakened before first light by one of the stranded sailors, who came rushing up from the beach.

"Awake! Awake," he shouted. "The pinnace! The pinnace!"

Ananias came from the bedroom, pulling on his breeches as he did. Shirtless and barefoot, he rushed out the door. I jumped from my day bed, glanced over to see that Valentyne was still asleep, and then went to the bedroom door. Elenora was sitting up, wearing nothing, lighting a candle.

"Go!" she said. "Go see what it is! I'll take care of the babies."

"Are you sure?"

"Go!"

I did, following Ananias out the door, barefoot and wearing only my shift. People appeared from the other cottages in various states of undress. Together, we ran to the shore in the dark.

From the beach, we could just make out the dark silhouette of the pinnace several hundred yards away. Her sail was raised and she was moving toward the pass in the barrier islands. "Where is she going?" we asked one another. "Who is aboard? Who knows anything about this?"

"It's the guv'nor and his men," answered one of the sailors. "Seen 'em with me own eyes. Came down quiet as mice, took a boat and rowed out. Then they hoisted and weighed, and there they go."

"Someone run back to the governor's house," commanded Ananias. "See if he's there."

It took less than five minutes for the runner to come back. It was true—John's house was empty. Ananias ordered the assistants who were on the beach—Roger Bailey and Thomas Stevens were two that I can recall specifically—to immediately take a census. "I want to know who is aboard with John White and who is not," said Ananias. "Everyone here is to gather in the community building so we can count heads."

Within the hour, we knew. John and six assistants were missing—the five who had stood with him in the two councils and Dyonis, who had not. Everyone else was accounted for.

"The bastards have abandoned us," said James Lasie to the gathered cluster of us.

"But where can they go?" asked someone else.

"Back to England, of course."

"The pinnace is not fitted out for a crossing," said one of the sailors. "They have no food or water. Surely they know that."

"Then what?"

No one knew. In the perplexed silence that followed, I could not help but wonder about Dyonis. Why was he among them?

"He is not one of them," Audry agreed. "And he is so incapacitated, why would they include him?"

What if they had not included him? The answer occurred to us both at the same time, and we quickly excused ourselves from the gathering and practically ran to Dyonis's house.

We called from the door and when we got no answer, we pushed open the door and went inside. The main room was empty. There was no sign that Dyonis had taken a meal—or done anything else—since the baby and I had moved out, and the curtain across the bedroom door was drawn.

Audry and I looked at each other. We each took a deep breath and drew it open.

Dyonis was there, lying on his back on the bed in a great pool of congealed blood, his two hands still gripping the knife he had plunged into his middle. His mouth was open and his dead eyes stared toward heaven.

"Oh, dear God," whispered Audry.

I could not even get that much out. My knees went weak and I clutched the door frame to stay upright. Audry put her arm around my shoulder and steered me out of the cottage, saying, "Go to the baby. I shall report this to the others." I nodded numbly and did as she'd said, shuffling across the village in something very close to a trance.

Inside Elenora's house, it was mercifully quiet. Valentyne was asleep in his little cot and so, apparently, were Elenora and Virginia in the bedroom. I carefully picked up tiny Valentyne, so as not to wake him, then sat down on my day bed and cradled him, rocking him gently back and forth while I tried not to cry.

"What are we going to do now, my little one?" I whispered. "What are we going to do?"

twenty—two

In the two days that followed John's theft of the pinnace, those of us who remained in the village got very little work done. Questions without answers hung in the air around us. Like the thick tendrils of gray moss that draped most of the trees outside our palisade, one could not proceed without being impeded by them. Where had John and the others gone? What would happen when the *Lyon* and the flyboat returned from offshore? If the pinnace never came back, how would that affect us?

And then there were the more immediately practical questions: With John and several assistants now gone, and with Dyonis and Margery now dead, who should move into their houses? And perhaps most important to me, who would care for baby Valentyne?

Before Ananias could organize us into a formal council to make any decisions, the pinnace returned. As before, word of it came from one of the stranded sailors, whose trained eye had spotted the tip of its approaching mast before the returning boat had cleared the inlet. We rushed to the beach.

Aboard the pinnace were Captain Stafford and a crew of sailors. As soon as our stranded sailors saw who it was, they let out a great huzzah, for they knew it meant that Simon and his two ships had weathered the dangerous storm and were now back at anchor outside the inlet.

When Captain Stafford and several of the crew rowed ashore to our beach, we were all amazed to see Christopher Cooper there, too. Once ashore, Stafford and Cooper asked to speak privately to Ananias and the other assistants, and we all stood watching as the group moved far enough down the beach to converse without being overheard.

"Cooper would not have come back without something important to say," said Audry at my side.

And as usual, Audry was right. After their short conference, the leaders called for an immediate council. We all streamed back inside the palisade and into the community building, where we were joined by those who had not been on the beach. I went to the Dares' cottage to pick up Valentyne, as well as Eleanora and Virginia, and together we carried the two babies to the council, where we stood with Audry in the back row of attendees.

"Who could possibly have guessed," said Audry, "that we all would travel halfway across the world just so we could gather and talk incessantly?"

"Not I," I answered. "But isn't this what we English do best?"

"Good point," said Audry. "But this is getting out of hand."

Ananias called the council to order and then turned control of the proceedings over to Christopher Cooper. "My friends," Cooper began, "your recent mutinous actions against your governor have forced him to seek shelter for his own safety."

"Not just him, sir!" shouted someone from the back of the room. "Include yourself and the other cowards who fled with him!" Others joined in the outcry.

Cooper raised his hands in acknowledgment. "Hear me out. Your fate may well hang in the balance." The room quieted.

"We are now aboard the flyboat and Governor White has assumed command of it," Cooper continued. "We intend to return to England and wash our hands of this entire enterprise. We will report the failure of the colony. You will never receive any resupply and you will all perish."

The room erupted in outrage. Again, Cooper asked to be heard, and continued.

"There is, however, an alternative. Neither the governor nor any of the assistants wish to lose the considerable investment in this enterprise. We also recognize that Sir Walter Raleigh will be greatly displeased should we be forced to report to him the loss of yet another colony here in Virginia. His displeasure will not bode well for us in England. It would be vastly preferable for us to report a successful planting of this colony and to arrange for its resupply. Thus, we are willing to arrange for that resupply—under certain circumstances."

"What circumstances?" Ananias demanded to know.

"The following, sir: We have drafted a document to be signed and sealed by every member of the colony, in which you affirm John White as the lawful governor of the colony and request that he return personally to England to arrange for its resupply. You acknowledge that the governor does this reluctantly and only upon the unanimous entreaty of the colony. Further, you affirm that you will vouchsafe to preserve and protect all the possessions and property that he has left here in your safekeeping, and will return the same to him upon his return as your lawful governor."

"'Tis extortion!" cried Thomas Hewet.

"Nay, sir. It is an arrangement of mutual interests. An offer of amnesty, if you will. And I urge you all to accept it."

The community broke down into many simultaneous discussions. I handed the sleeping Valentyne to Audry, then pushed to the front and raised my voice.

"Master Cooper, you made no mention of Simon Fernandez," I said. "Is he aware of this arrangement?" The room quieted to hear his answer.

"An excellent question, Mrs. Merrimoth. He is indeed aware, and he approves. Governor White dined with him aboard the *Lyon* last evening. At that meeting, the governor explained that he and all you colonists had settled your differences and the request that you will now sign was already in agreement. Simon was quite pleased to hear this, for it allowed him to immediately set sail—which he did at first light this morning. The *Lyon,* ladies and gentlemen, has left the new world."

My heart sank. Not only had I hoped Simon might save us from John's self-serving plot, but I had always assumed that I would see Simon at least one more time before he left for England. I thought I still had the chance, however unlikely it was that I might take it, to change my mind and return with him. Not now. Without another word, I stepped back.

"He has the upper hand completely," Audry said. "We will have to accept. It's dastardly, but quite clever."

Her assessment was not unique. Though many voiced outrage and disapproval, none could offer argument against accepting John's terms. In the end, we all agreed. A table was carried to the center of the community building and the document set thereupon, along with a quill pen and bottle of ink. Ananias and Christopher Cooper sat at the table to observe. We then lined up, one by one, to set our hands to the blank page at the end of the document. When it came my turn, I hesitated. Here was a last chance to say something to John, by passing a note to him via Christopher Cooper.

"Yes, Mrs. Merrimoth?" Cooper asked.

I shook my head. "Nothing."

I signed my name and walked away. Not since the death of my good second husband had I felt so suddenly alone and abandoned. I took Valentyne from Audry and walked back to Elenora's house. At least there was that to look forward to—my milk was beginning to come in.

twenty—three

Not long after I had retired with Elenora to her house to feed the two babies, Ananias also returned. Both Elenora and I were nursing.

"Cooper and Captain Stafford are preparing to return to the flyboat," he said. "They have offered to carry with them any tokens or messages that any of us may have for anyone back home in England."

For a moment, Elenora and Ananias looked at each other without speaking. They did not have to explain to me the question that hung in the air between them: Did Elenora wish to send a message to her father, John White? Finally, she just shook her head. There were tears in her eyes.

Ananias nodded, then turned to me. "Emme?"

I, too, shook my head. He turned to leave. "I do have a question, though," I added.

Valentyne began to fuss. He had gotten what little I had for him on my right side, so I turned him to feed on the left, a procedure that left me more than a little exposed to Ananias until I had resettled the baby and could cover myself again.

"How can we be certain that they will keep their side of the arrangement?" I asked.

"A fair question," Ananias noted. "And the answer, of course, is that we do not. Though it seems in their best interest to do so."

"May I make a suggestion?"

"By all means," he said.

"The document we have all just signed . . . is Christopher Cooper to carry it back to the flyboat in person?"

"Of course. Why do you ask?"

"Might they be more inclined to return with supplies if one of their own were to remain here with us?"

Ananias folded his hands. "Of course. Of course." A slow smile came to his face and he gave me a little bow. "Thank you, Emme. I am embarrassed not to have thought of that myself. I shall take some pleasure in informing Assistant Cooper that his continuing services are required here in Virginia until such time as our relief supplies are delivered from England." He turned and strode from the house.

Little Virginia was full and had fallen asleep. Elenora stood up and carried her into the bedroom to set her down in her cot.

"That was quite a clever thought," said Elenora as she walked back into the main room. "Whose was it?"

"Whose was it?"

"Of course it wasn't yours. Who whispered it to you? Audry? Or one of your men?"

I held back. This was her house and Ananias was her husband. She had just given birth and was saddled with an additional baby that, though I was trying, I had not yet weaned from her. We had both seen the way Ananias looked at me. Elenora had every reason to be curt. God knows I certainly would have been, had the tables been turned.

Valentyne began to fuss again. He needed more. I stood and handed him to Elenora, then refastened my dress while she took a long, slow breath and began to feed him.

"I won't be in your way much longer, Elenora," I said. "I really won't."

Outside, people were moving in groups back down to the beach. I followed, falling in with Arnold and Joyce Archard and their seven-year-old son, Thomas, who kept skipping ahead, chafing at the adult pace we maintained in the midafternoon heat.

"Have you found a suitable housing arrangement yet, Emme?" asked Joyce. She, Arnold, and Thomas shared a cottage with Ambrose and Elizabeth Viccars and their six-year-old, Ambrose Jr. The two couples had also taken in young George Howe after his father's death. It had seemed best to put the young boys under the same roof, where they could be watched by one of the mothers while the other went about her work. So far, the arrangement seemed to be working.

"No," I answered, "but I dare say I'll not be adding to the circus in yours."

They both laughed. "A plan will be made soon enough," said Arnold. "The Dares will move into the governor's house, that seems certain. And I see no reason why you and the Harvey infant cannot stay in that house, along with one or two others who could certainly move there, as well."

"That would suit me," I said. "I wouldn't want to take up a whole cottage when others must still share their smaller spaces."

"Quite," said Joyce.

At the beach, the pinnace was about to set off for the flyboat. Aboard were Captain Stafford, all of the remaining stranded sailors, and a small party of our own men who would bring the pinnace back. Notably absent was Christopher Cooper. He was standing apart, held at bay by John Hynde and William Clement, both of whom had pistols in their hands. Both had spent time in Colchester Prison and were hard men; I doubted the firearms were needed. Ananias had chosen his deputies well. Master Cooper was going nowhere and, by the deflated look on his face, he knew it.

twenty-four

Late August in England is when the summer heat begins to abate, and the same is true here in the new world. The difference is that there is no actual cooling here, just a reduction from unbearable to merely uncomfortable. The relief was much welcome during the days following the departure of the ships for England, as summer became fall.

The change was evident in more than the weather. With John and his dissidents now gone, and with Ananias our uncontested leader, we were all able to turn our energies to making our community the permanent settlement we wanted it to be. Gardens were tended, cottages made more comfortable, and our palisade restored to its full strength.

In the nearby waters, Manteo and his men showed some of our men how to use fresh-cut sticks to construct clever mazes in the shallows into which schools of fish would swim and become entrapped, making it easy for our men to spear them by the basketful. The native women showed us English women how to dry the resultant bounty, so that we would have fish to eat throughout the winter. Some of us even began to learn a few Indian words. Audry was particularly adept, and she in turn taught some of our words to them.

It was a bit odd, clad in our long dresses and working side by side with the Indian women, who were all but naked, but we became used to it. The same disparity in attire was true of our men working with Manteo and his men out on the water, but the men were able to adjust by doffing their shirts. I, for one, was envious of that, recalling from the island of Caykos how good it had felt to be naked in the water under the hot sun. When the two of us were alone, I even told Audry about that excursion.

"You did not!" she exclaimed. "Emme!"

All I could do was shrug. And all she could do in return was to shake her head.

During that same week, we also reallocated the village houses. As Arnold Archard had predicted, Ananias and Elenora moved into the governor's house with little Virginia. I was assigned to Dyonis and Margery's cottage with Valentyne, along with three of the other single women, Jane Pierce, Margaret Lawrence, and Agnes Wood. Jane and Margaret were widows several years older than I, and Agnes was but seventeen. All three had joined the colony from different backgrounds but with similar purpose: to find a husband from among the colonists. Though none of them cared to discuss details, it was apparent that all three, like me, had good reason to leave England and very little to call them back. In good time, I assumed, we would gain enough comfort with one another for them to be more forthcoming.

As for my being given custody of Valentyne, nothing was formally decreed. But now that my milk was in full flow, I was able to feed him on my own, and with three other women in the cottage with me, the baby lacked not for care or attention. No one in the colony voiced any objection, and so I became Valentyne's adoptive mother by unspoken consent.

This happy state of affairs continued for a few weeks. The oppressive summer heat lingered through September. Our gardens matured nicely, thanks mostly to the plants from Wanchese's abandoned village that we had so laboriously replanted. Meat was plentiful, as our hunters learned from Manteo's men the best places to find bear and deer, of which there seemed an endless supply. Flocks of migrating waterbirds filled the nearby shallows and were easy to shoot. While we plucked and cleaned them, the Indian women told us with shakes of their heads and much pointing to the north that this was nothing, that many more flocks were yet to come. It did begin to appear that the glowing stories we had all heard back in England might actually be true.

To celebrate the beginning of harvest time, someone—I cannot now recall who it was—suggested that we use the community building for its real purpose, to mount a feast complete with dancing. The idea quickly spread. A date was set, invitations were passed to Manteo and his people, and one night at the end of September, the event took place.

We worked all day to set up. Pits were dug and fires started early for spit-roasted deer and bear. Breads were baked, sweets unpacked, beverages prepared. One of our two remaining casks of beer was allocated for the festivities. Arriving at midday, the Indians brought with them baskets of victuals and earthen containers of their wine. There were two dozen or so people who made the journey by canoe from Croatoan, about evenly divided between men and women, and including Benginoor and Manteo.

"Do you think the Indians will dance?" asked Audry while we were arranging tables and benches.

"I have no idea," I answered. "But if their women do in that state of undress, methinks some of our men would trip over themselves to join their circle."

"'Twill be an interesting evening, no doubt."

And that it was. In our zeal to mount the celebration, it had occurred to none of us to ask whether or not there were musicians among us. It turned out that we had none save poor Richard Tomkins, a shy clerk who had brought with him the only instrument in our colony, a strange new stringed instrument called a fiddle that he had no skill in playing. When pressed into demonstrating, the sound was akin to a cat screeching and we all shook our heads and told him to put it away.

"We'll have to do with clapping, then," said Elizabeth Viccars. "Because I for one look forward to several rounds of 'Jenny Pluck Pears.'"

"Not to mention 'Cuckolds All in a Row' for your husband, then," said Joyce Archard. The two were fast friends and we all laughed.

The feast itself went as planned. Starting late in the afternoon, it continued through the courses that we had all cooked. People mingled at different tables with none of the societal hierarchy one might have seen back in England. Even the Indians joined in the mixing, though perhaps not quite as fluidly as did we. No one would start dancing until later in the evening.

Because I had Valentyne to care for, I came and went from the festivities. The cottage I now shared with the three other women was near enough to the community building that I felt comfortable leaving the baby in his cot whenever he went back to sleep after feeding. And on those times when he stayed awake and alert, I carried him back to the feast with me, where he tried to take in the sights and sounds with his new blue eyes. He was, of course, a great attraction, especially to the Indian women, who seemed fascinated by him. I gladly handed Valentyne to any who asked to hold him, an act that seemed purely natural to me, but which drew disapproving looks from some of the Englishwomen. Elenora, I noticed, kept Virginia tightly locked in her own arms and shied away when any of the Croatoan women approached her.

As was his wont, Valentyne fell fast asleep after his evening feeding. Young Agnes told me she was shy about the prospect of dancing and wanted to stay in our cottage. "I will listen for him," she said. "You go and enjoy yourself."

"You won't find a husband that way," I said.

She blushed a bright crimson and then gave herself away by glancing toward the back door. Whoever was hiding there shuffled his feet.

I laughed. "I'd best be on my way, then."

Back in the community building, the celebration seemed to have truly begun. Four couples had started a circle dance. The others surrounded them and clapped to set the steps, as the dancers swirled, hooked elbows, and changed partners. Elsewhere, people sat at tables conversing. Food and drink were still in ample supply.

Manteo, Benginoor, and several others from Croatoan were sitting together, and when Benginoor looked my way and smiled, I joined them. Benginoor surprised me by greeting me in broken English.

"God evenik, merry mot," she said in the same singsong rhythm that Manteo used.

"And good evening to you, Benginoor," I said. "You have been learning English."

She smiled and canted her head toward Manteo.

"A little," he said. "I have been giving her instruction, but it does not come quickly, as it did not come quickly to me."

"Tell her I look forward to the day when I can converse with her, woman to woman."

She laughed when Manteo translated, then gave him a reply. "Yes," said Manteo. "She says she would like that very much. She would ask you about me. She would ask how her son behaved among the English women."

"You can tell her that around this Englishwoman, her son was the very soul of a gentleman." She smiled and nodded her head to me when he translated.

"Even when we were naked together," I added.

Manteo's eyes widened and he shook his head. Benginoor clearly asked him what I had said. He then answered in their language. She laughed and responded. All the Indians at the table laughed.

"That is the most important time to be a gentleman," he translated.

"Only if the lady wants him to be," I answered with a smile. All the Indians erupted with very loud laughter when Manteo translated.

The merriment at our table drew several others from the colony. Soon, Manteo was very busy translating banter back and forth. It was most enjoyable for us all and contributed in no small way to extending the festivities further into the evening hours. More dancers joined the others and louder rhythmic clapping filled the air. A few of the Indians, beginning with a few of the men, were eventually cajoled into trying to match the steps in one of our country dances, and picked it up quite quickly. Several of their women then joined in, and soon there were three circles of dancers twirling and bumping into each other, as everyone urged one another on with rhythmic claps and loud laughter, especially whenever someone tripped over another's missed step and fell down in the happy melee.

In the middle of this dance fest, Ananias tapped me on the arm and asked me to join one of the circles with him. Why not? I shrugged, and soon we were in the midst of it. And what a scene it was, especially when one was a part of it! No one seemed to know which dance we were each attempting, so there was no uniform call to twirl, to change directions or, for that matter, to change partners. It all happened on the fly, and was rendered doubly strange when one was twirled away from one's properly clad English partner into the loose embrace of a nearly naked Indian, man or woman. And then there was the constant vision of their bare dancing buttocks interspersed with our flying skirts and spinning male breeches, all while one was fast-stepping and nearly out of breath. If any of us colonists still had any doubts about this being a new world, they were now erased.

When the dancing came to a natural pause, Ananias escorted me back toward the table where Elenora and several others were sitting. Little Virginia was still up, fussing slightly in Elenora's arms. As Ananias and I approached, still flushed and exhilarated from our dancing, Elenora directed at me as dark and accusatory a look as I had received in a very long time—so dark, in fact, that I simply turned away and returned to Manteo's and Benginoor's table. I was having too much fun to settle under Elenora's jealous cloud, especially when there was no cause. During our dancing, Ananias and I had rarely been anywhere near each other. If Elenora wanted someone to accuse of any impropriety, she would have done much better to fix her angry gaze on any one of the bare-breasted Indian women whose gyrating but-tocks had drawn considerably more attention from her husband than had anything I could offer in competition.

With Manteo and Benginoor, things were considerably more convivial. Through Manteo, Benginoor told me that she would be staying overnight at Manteo's hut here on Roanoke Island and invited me to visit her there the next morning.

"We talk again," she said on her own. "Bring baby. Bring friend." She pointed to Audry.

"I will," I answered. "Thank you."

I then excused myself and returned home, knowing it would soon be time to feed Valentyne. Along the way, I could see several shadowy couples moving off together toward more private spots, including one or two of our men with their arms around Indian women. Back at the cottage, Agnes sat alone demurely with no sign of her secret suitor. I thanked her for watching the baby without commenting on the fact that her dress had not been fully relaced.

After I fed Valentyne and put him back to bed, it took me a very long time to fall asleep. And when I finally did, my head was filled with dreams the content of which I shall not put down in this journal.

As Audry had predicted, it had indeed been an interesting evening. Although I could not know, it was also the last one I would spend inside the walls of the Citie of Raleigh for a very long time.

twenty-five

The path from our palisade-surrounded village to Manteo's hut was
not directly along the shore—which would have been shorter—but
instead followed the natural contour of the inland forest, avoiding
wetland and sand dune alike to provide good, dry footing at any time
of year. The path was almost two miles and had evidently been in use
for many years, dating back to a time before any of us English had
arrived. It was said that the people of Wanchese's band had made a
seasonal fishing and hunting camp where our village now stood, but
that had ended as the bad blood between Manteo's people and his had
escalated into frequent fighting.

On the morning that Audry and I walked the path, we were
accompanied by John Wright, who had been with the previous expedition and was thus familiar with the route, and Roger Bailey, one of
the assistants. Ananias had sent both men along with us when Audry
and I asked his permission to skip our chores in order to accept Benginoor's invitation. Audry's husband, Thomas, had been too engaged

with his own work in the busy forge to join us, but, of course, we needed armed escorts to venture outside the palisade. That requirement still stood, though Wanchese and his men had fled from their village across the bay. It was a sensible enough caution and both John and Roger were more than happy to break their normal routines to accompany us on what amounted to little more than an enjoyable walk in the forest.

The walk took no more than half an hour, short enough so that it was no burden to carry Valentyne the whole way. The baby kept his eyes open the entire time, looking up. It must have been quite magical to his little eyes, trying to make sense of the shifting colors and shapes as we passed under the tall green trees and the bright blue sky far above.

Manteo had chosen his hut's site well, placing it just inland from the beach on a small rise, allowing for an open view across the water to the mainland, four or five miles away. The hut itself was rectangular and larger than I expected it to be, occupying as much ground space as one of our larger cottages in the village. Like those in his town on Croatoan, it had no windows, just woven mats that formed its walls. Today, the mats were rolled up to reveal the interior, where Manteo and Benginoor were sitting together. As soon as the four of us came into sight, they came out to greet us.

"Interesting that their queen and chief man let us approach unchallenged like this," remarked Roger. "Armed as we are."

"They did not," said John. "Look behind."

On the path behind us were four Indians carrying bows and arrows. Manteo waved his arm at them and they vanished as silently as they had appeared.

"Impressive," said Roger.

John nodded. "'Tis their way. They will sit for hours watching a path. Nothing goes unobserved."

"Hall-o!" said Benginoor, smiling as always. "Come, fren." She waved us into the hut.

Here, I dearly wish that I could write an account of a pleasant conversation among friends getting to know one another better. I think that was our shared intention. But before we even had a chance to exchange pleasantries, Manteo's men in the forest shouted a warning, and Audry's husband, Thomas, appeared on the path just moments later, unarmed and out of breath. He appeared to have run all the way from the village.

We all rushed out to meet him, I with Valentyne still in my arms.

Thomas was so winded that at first he could not even speak. "Please!" said Audry. "What is it?"

He held up a hand, took several hard breaths, and then gasped it out: "It's Elenora . . . She . . . has found . . . drawings."

"Drawings?" said Audry.

"By her . . . father . . . of Emme and . . ." He looked at me and then at Manteo. "And of you, sir."

Manteo and I looked at each other. Audry looked back and forth between her husband and Manteo and me. We said nothing. John Wright and Roger Bailey were as perplexed as Audry. Finally Audry threw her hands in the air. "Will somebody explain this to me?"

"John is an artist," I said. "He made pictures of me."

"So?"

"In the nude."

"Oh."

"Who has she shown them to?" I asked Thomas.

"Everyone," answered Thomas. "She has tacked them to the community building wall. The entire village has seen them. There is a great uproar."

"Why?" demanded Audry. "Surely we are not that prudish."

"One of them is . . . scandalous." Thomas looked at me and at Manteo. The others then did, as well.

"What?" said Audry. "Tell me."

"There is one drawing of Manteo and me together," I said. "On the Caykos islands, when we both bathed."

Audry's eyes went wide. "And you are both . . . ?" She turned to Thomas. "And they are both . . . ?" He nodded, and she turned back to me. "Oh, Emme," she said. "What have you done?"

"It was perfectly innocent," I argued. "We went into the water and bathed separately. Afterward, John asked us to stand together while he made his drawing. Then we dressed and returned to the *Lyon*. Is that not right, Manteo?"

He nodded. "That is right."

Audry's face hardened. The expressions on the faces of Thomas, John, and Roger were equally grim.

"No," she said. "You are both wrong. That is not right. And that has not been perfectly innocent since Adam and Eve were still in the Garden." She fixed her gaze on me. "I am disappointed. I should have known better."

"We must all go back now," said Thomas. "Many were calling for an immediate council and there is sure to be one." He took Audry by the arm and turned away. John and Roger followed. I, too, started in that direction.

"Wait," said Manteo. We all stopped. "Mrs. Merrimoth should not go. She must stay here."

"No," said Roger. As assistant, he was the senior Englishman there. "She must come back with us."

"No," said Manteo, quite forcefully this time. "She must not. Your people do not understand. They will mistreat her."

"That, sir, is for us to decide."

"I am governor here. It is for me to decide."

The three Englishmen looked at each other, then each nodded. "As you wish, sir," said Roger.

They left. As she walked away, Audry looked at me over her shoulder. I wanted to wave or shrug or make some sign to her, but I could not. Valentyne was in my arms. Audry shook her head at me and kept walking.

twenty-six

I spent the rest of the evening in conversation with Manteo and Bengi-noor. Both wanted to try to understand why the English reacted with such outrage at the pictures made by John. It was not easy to explain. Benginoor kept trying to understand what "innocent" meant. I tried to explain it in terms of good and evil, but Benginoor kept shaking her head the way one does when there are too many flies buzzing near one's ears.

"What garden?" she abruptly asked.

"What garden?" I answered.

"You fren say 'not since garden,' when say Manteo wrong."

"Oh, yes. The Garden of Eden. It is where the first two people lived. Adam and Eve. They were naked there. That's what Audry meant."

Benginoor listened as Manteo translated.

"No robe in Garden is innocent?" she asked me. "But no robe here is not?"

"Yes. Adam and Eve did not know good and evil. They were innocent. But then they sinned. After that they were no longer innocent, so God cast them out of the Garden. Since then, no one has been innocent. We are all sinners."

"Explain 'sinner.'"

I paused for thought. "Sin is when a person does a thing forbidden by God."

Benginoor and Manteo both nodded.

"Understand," Benginoor said. "We believe that, too." Then she squinted. "No robe forbidden by your God?"

I took a breath. Audry was a tutor. She could have handled questions like these, not me.

"Not directly," I answered. "But no robe is immodest. Immodesty is a sin."

She nodded. "Not to us. But to you?"

I nodded. "That is the problem with the pictures. My people say they show me being immodest. They say they show me committing a sin."

After Manteo translated, we were quiet. Valentyne fussed and I picked him up.

"Where is Garden?" Benginoor asked me. "In England?"

I laughed. "England is far from the Garden of Eden. No one knows where it is. God took it away when Adam and Eve sinned."

"Maybe here." She smiled. "We still no robe. We still innocent."

"Yes." I smiled back. "Maybe here. Why not here?"

"Not here," said Manteo abruptly. We both looked at him. Apart from translating for his mother and me as we spoke, he had said little. Now he spoke directly to us both, first to his mother in their language and then to me in English, alternating as he did.

"Not here because we are not innocent. We do sin. We fight and kill each other, just as in England. Not here because we punish people for doing things we do not understand, just as in England. Here is no Garden of Eden, just as England is not."

There was little to say after that. Together we sat in silence until full darkness fell, after which we retired to our mats for the night. I curled up on mine with Valentyne held close to keep him warm. For a long time I lay that way, listening to the soft sounds he made in his sleep and trying to imagine the babe's new world, the one he would find when he, too, grew old enough to see it for what it was.

twenty—seven

Early the next morning a deputation of colonists arrived at Manteo's hut. Among them were both Christopher Cooper and Elizabeth Glane, so I knew before their intention was even announced that they were here to denounce me.

Christopher Cooper took the lead, producing a document from which he read:

"May it please you, Governor Manteo and fellow citizens of Virginia residing in Croatoan and elsewhere, we, your friends and fellow citizens of Virginia residing in the Citie of Raleigh, do by these presents seek custody of Emme Merrimoth for the purpose of transporting her back to the Citie, so that she may be made to stand trial on a charge of witchcraft. In addition, we seek return of the infant Valentyne Harvey, which infant was unlawfully taken by said Emme Merrimoth from its rightful home within the Citie. Signed and sealed this twenty-third day of September in the year of Our Lord one thousand five hundred eighty-seven."

Cooper then handed the document to Manteo, who read it slowly and carefully. He then handed it back to Cooper.

"No," he said.

"Sir!" exclaimed Cooper. It came out more as a wheeze and whine than an actual word. "This is a lawful demand!"

"It is a demand, yes. Lawful, no. I am the governor. For it to be lawful, I must sign it."

"Then, good sir, please sign it."

"I will not."

"Why not?"

"Because I have been to England. In England I have seen one of your witch trials. I have seen the people cheering when the woman was hanged. I do not care to see such a thing again. And I will not allow it here."

"Sir—"

"Silence!" Manteo looked down at Cooper. Neither Cooper nor any of the others who had accompanied him said a word.

"Now," said Manteo. "The question of the infant is separate. Go back to your village and rewrite your demand for his return. Make clear your reasons why I should grant that request. When it is so written, please have Ananias Dare himself come and make the argument. I and my mother will hear that argument, and will then decide whether the infant remains here with Mrs. Merrimoth or is returned to the people of your village."

There was no choice but compliance. Leaving behind only the lingering hatred I saw in the eyes of Elizabeth Glane, the colonists turned away and headed back on the path to the village. Manteo then turned to me.

"Emme," he said, "you must prepare your argument for keeping the infant in your care."

"Is that really necessary?" I asked. "Is it not obvious?"

Manteo shook his head. "It is not," he said. "You are not the baby's mother. There has been no formal adoption. It is a fair question."

He turned to go. I stopped him with two questions. "How is it that you know our law so well?" I asked. "Is it so similar to your own?"

He shook his head. "I studied it while I was in England, because it is so different. I knew that if we were to live together here, your people and mine would have to choose which rules to live by. That is what I am trying to do here today."

For a moment we looked at each other. "I hope you choose well," I said.

"I know you do."

I will leave it to each reader of this journal to decide whether or not Manteo chose well, for as everyone still living in the village now knows, Ananias and Elenora came with a new delegation to make their argument for the return of Valentyne to them. I tried to argue that I had been a good mother to him, that I now loved him as much as if I had birthed him, but to no avail. Manteo awarded custody to Ananias and Elenora themselves. Elenora stepped forward and I handed Valentyne to her. Neither of us said a word.

Manteo then gave a short speech, reminding everyone that he was governor. He stated again that there was to be no witch trial, that I was a free colonist, the same as any of them, and there would be no action taken against me or any other citizen of Virginia without his authority. He even asked them to verify that they understood by saying "aye." Some grudgingly, others defiantly, maybe even a few in quiet agreement, they all agreed.

The whole unhappy affair took less than an hour. The colonists then returned to the village, taking Valentyne with them. With their departure, the Indians began packing up their cooking pots and other things. The warriors who had been watching from the forest came back and carried everything to the canoes on the beach.

I did not help. All I could do was watch silently, trying hard not to cry. Finally, Benginoor came over and put her arm around my shoulder.

"Come," she said. "We go."

I shook my head. "I stay here."

"No," she said. "All go."

"No. You go. I stay."

She pursed her lips, shook her head, and walked away. She soon returned, this time with Manteo.

"My mother says you wish to stay here."

"Yes. I would like to be alone."

"You have no food."

"I am not hungry. When I need to eat, I will go to the citie."

He considered this. "We will leave you food and water. Two of my men will stay here to look after you. They will sleep in the forest and will not disturb you unless you call for them. Do not go back to the citie until I return to accompany you."

I nodded. I wasn't sure I would go back even then.

An hour later, I stood on the beach and waved as the canoes paddled away. Benginoor waved back. Behind me on the bank, the two Indian men watched for a time, and then vanished silently. I was alone. Only when the canoes were far enough away so that I knew they could not see me do it, I sat down on the beach and started to cry.

twenty-eight

That night, as I tried to sleep in Manteo's hut, the summer heat came back. Each hour seemed hotter and more humid than the last. I doubt that I would have been able to sleep, regardless, but the heat made it impossible. In addition to the close, sticky air, there was the growing discomfort from not having nursed in so many hours and my anxiety at being alone and without Valentyne. I repeatedly stood and paced, and then lay back down and tried once again to doze off. It was too hot, even after I had shed all of my clothing. Nothing worked.

Sometime in the middle of the night, I got up and went outside. The stars were bright, though muted through the humid haze. I walked down to the beach, folding my arms under my aching breasts to keep them from jostling too much, and when I got to the shoreline, I kept walking. The sand beneath the water was soft on my feet, though the water was so warm that I could barely tell I was even in it. Only the tickling circle of the surface as it rose up my torso and the soft resistance as I moved through it told me I was indeed walking in water. I kept going, until I was in up to my breasts. The support of the water was so soothing, I was able to unfold my arms, and I stood that way for a long time, relishing the relief.

Turning to the north, I found Stella Maris. As I had with Simon on the stern deck of the anchored *Lyon,* I turned west and looked at the darkened smudge that was the mainland, five miles across the bay. Somewhere over there were Wanchese and his people, but tonight I felt no anxiety about them. My more immediate problems were so much closer.

I turned around and started walking back, and that's when I again saw the sparkling glow of phosphor, just as I had in the middle of the ocean in the wake of the *Lyon.* Now it radiated out from me as I moved through the shallow water. I dragged my hand and it trailed behind my fingers like a thousand tiny stars tumbling in their wake before slowly twinkling out in the black water. I walked back to the beach doing that, leaving eddies of little fading stars behind me, and wondering if John or Simon might right now be seeing the same thing tumbling behind them, on their separate ways back to England.

I never did fall asleep that night. Back at the hut, all I could do was sit inside the rolled-up siding and wait for dawn. As the light slowly grew, the nearby trees took shape, first as only jagged edges where their tops met the lightening sky, and then more fully discernible, as their colors slowly made themselves known in the gathering daylight. It was going to be so very hot, I thought about not putting my dress back on. Now that I was living like an Indian, why not go as naked as they did? But I could not make myself do it. I got dressed and laced myself up tight in front, trying to offset the increasing pain from the lack of nursing. I wondered what was to be done if it kept getting worse.

My second baby had been just a few weeks older than Valentyne when she caught the fever and died, and the same thing had happened then. My near neighbor Grace and I had tried to hand express my milk then, but we could not get enough out to alleviate the pain—in fact, it had made the discomfort worse. The only thing to do was to find a baby to suckle at my breast, but there was not an infant in the area. Eventually, Grace tentatively offered to do it herself, as long as neither of us ever spoke of it. I agreed and so she did. It did help. We had not been good friends and parted company afterward. I had little hope of finding the same relief here.

The day was long, hot, and terribly uncomfortable for me. By late afternoon, I would have again allowed a friend to relieve me. I had tried to express the milk myself with my own hands, but, as before, I could not get enough out and the squeezing only increased the pain. It was hard to think about anything else. Just as I was deciding it might be near dark enough for me to undress and return to the water, one of the Indians came out of the woods and called to me. With gestures toward the path he made himself understood: Someone was coming.

It was Ananias. The Indians stopped him as he got to the clearing. I waved to them that it was all right. They let him pass and disappeared once again. I looked behind Ananias, expecting more colonists, but he was alone.

"What are you doing here?" I asked, as soon as he was near enough.

"I am looking for Manteo. Where is he?" He was dripping with perspiration from his hot walk through the forest.

"Gone back to Croatoan with the others."

He looked around. "You are here alone?"

"In this house, yes. You saw my guardians."

He looked back to where they had stopped him. "Where are they now?"

"They stay in the forest. Why do you seek Manteo?"

"Governance business. When will he return?"

A sudden clap of thunder startled us both. To the west the sky was filled with boiling purple clouds, coming rapidly in our direction. Lightning flashed, followed a few seconds later by another clap of thunder.

"Come inside," I said. "Quickly."

We both did, just ahead of the storm. The day turned almost as dark as night. Rain and wind rattled against the roof in wild, continuous sheets. Lightning and thunder came almost nonstop as we struggled to lower the rolled-up siding mats and tie them down, and we both got drenched with rainwater in the process. The lowered mats bent and bowed under the lash of the storm, but they kept out the rain and let in only a few small gusts of wind. The hut was now surprisingly weather-tight. Wet, exhilarated, and unable to speak over the din of the storm, we stood looking at each other in the dim hut, our faces lit by sudden flashes of light while deafening thunder roiled outside. Ananias took a step toward me. I stepped back.

"No," I said, my voice so lost in the roar of the storm I could barely hear myself.

He tried to take me in his arms, but I pushed away. He caught me and pulled me hard against him. I cried out in pain and he let go immediately. "What?"

It hurt so much I had trouble speaking. I bent over and folded my arms under my breasts, then walked over and sat down on one of the benches.

He followed and squatted down in front of me, his face pursed in concern. "What is it?"

"My breasts. They hurt. From not . . ."

"From not . . . ?"

"Nursing."

"I'm sorry. I didn't know."

"You wouldn't."

The thunder, lightning, and wind continued unreduced. Not only was I hurting, but in the draftiness of the hut, I now felt a chill from my soaking dress. Ananias sat down beside me and put his arm around my shoulders. I leaned into him for the body heat that passed quickly through our wet garments.

"Cannot anything be done?" he asked.

"You could bring my baby back to me."

"He is not yours, Emme."

128

"Tell that to my overfilled breasts."

He did not answer. What could he know about it? He pulled me closer and I pushed him away.

"Did I not feed him?" I said. "Did I not give him nourishment and care? Did I not love him? Do I not ache to feed him again? To hold him again?"

"Emme, what am I to say? The decision was not mine to make alone."

I took a moment to calm myself. "I know," I finally said. And then, so quickly that I had not time to try to stop myself, I burst into tears. "It just hurts so much!" I blubbered. "It's more than I can bear! Can't you see that? Can't you?"

"Yes," he said. "I can."

I kept crying, unable to stop. He looked at me with genuine concern. Then he began to unlace my dress.

"What are you doing?" I said.

"What has to be done."

"No."

He finished unlacing and opened the front of my dress. He moved from the bench and got on his knees in front of me. He looked up at me. "Yes or no?" he said.

The pain was excruciating. I nodded.

Very tentatively, he began. Nothing came. He looked back up at me. "Harder?" he asked. I nodded. He tried again, with more suction.

"Too hard," I quickly said.

On the third try, he got it just right. He looked up at me in surprise. "'Tis sweeter than I had thought," he said.

"'Tis for babies," I reminded him.

He continued, and so did the storm. As lightning flashed and thunder rolled, Ananias slowly and patiently drew the pain from first one of my breasts and then the other. Neither of us spoke. I barely moved. As the discomfort drained from my body, it was replaced with such lassitude and relief that I felt as if I might faint. Finally, when he'd finished, I lay back on the bench, dreamy and carried away. It was

129

quite unlike any sensation I had ever felt—in truth, it was the very absence of any sensation at all. Not even the continuing lightning and overpowering thunder could rouse me from my reverie.

Ananias stayed by my side, sitting on the floor next to the bench. He laid his head on my bare midriff, his face toward mine as I lay on my back on the bench. He began to stroke my breasts.

"They are much softer now," he said.

I answered without opening my eyes. "Thanks to you." I put my hand on top of his as his hands continued moving over my chest.

He took my hand and lightly kissed it. "Now I have a favor to ask of you," he said.

"Anything," I said.

"I want you to relieve me."

I said nothing.

"Elenora has not allowed me since we left England," he continued.

"She was with child. The voyage was difficult for her."

"Both are well in the past." He let go of my hand and returned to caressing my breasts. "She does not even allow my hands to touch her like this. It has been months. My need matches yours, Emme."

"I was in pain. You ask too much."

"I ask no more than I gave to you."

I knew this was not an argument I was going to win, not alone with him in this place with my bare breasts already in his hands. I pushed him away and stood up.

"All right," I said. My hair had come loose and some had fallen across my face. I pushed it back into place. "You comforted me with your mouth. I can do the same for you."

A very bright bolt of lightning lit the hut's whole interior, freezing the quizzical look on his face.

"Yes or no, Ananias? I will not offer you more."

"Yes," he said.

In his state of need, it did not take long. Afterward, we sat side by side on the bench and said little. The storm continued and in our wet clothes we both grew more chilled. Ananias stood up and began to look among the baskets and pottery of the hut.

"What are you looking for?" I asked.

"I see there is a stack of firewood here," he answered, continuing his search. "Aha," he exclaimed, peering into an earthen pot. "Here are his fire-making supplies."

He brought out tinder and a friction bow and started a fire in the ring of stones in the center of the hut. The flames caught and it grew smoky inside with the mats rolled down, but the hut was not so tight as to hold it all. Enough escaped so that the smoke never got so thick as to make one cough. As soon as the warmth began to spread, Ananias took off his wet clothes and hung them close to the fire. I then did the same. After what we had just done for each other, why remain clothed, chilled, and uncomfortable?

Now we were both hungry. In other containers we found dried fish and other victuals. We sat near the fire and ate, as the storm slowly abated. To an outside observer, we would surely have looked like an Indian husband and wife, naked and eating with our bare hands. By the time we finished our supper, it was fully dark outside but still raining. Lightning continued, though sporadically, and thunder still rumbled. It was plain that Ananias would have to spend the night in the hut, rather than attempt the walk back to the village.

I was exhausted, since I had not slept in two days. I showed Ananias where to find an additional sleeping mat and watched as he placed it next to the fire, then unrolled my own on the opposite side, lay down upon it, and almost instantly fell asleep.

Sometime in the night, I awoke. The fire had burned down completely and I was shivering with cold. From his stirring, I could tell that Ananias, too, was awake on his mat on the other side of the now-cold fire ring. The rain had stopped, but the lightning and thunder continued, farther away and less intense.

"Are you cold?" he asked.

"Yes. Aren't you?"

"I am." He got up and felt our garments as they hung. "Still wet," he said.

He picked up his mat and brought it around to my side of the fire ring, spread it on the ground and then lay down next to me. I turned my back to him. He curled around me and put his arm across my shoulders, but we both continued to shiver. We pressed closer together, and it soon worked—I stopped shivering, grew sleepy again, and fell back to sleep.

I awoke in pain. We were still curled together, though Ananias had cupped one of my breasts and when he pulled me closer, it hurt. I moved his hand away. He put it on my other breast and I winced and pushed it away again. He shifted away from me and I rolled onto my back.

"The same?" he asked.

"Not as bad," I replied.

"But painful again?"

"Yes."

He propped himself up on his elbow, then brought his mouth down to my breast.

"Ananias, you don't—"

He shushed me.

As before, he slowly took the pain away, first from my left side and then from my right. And just as before, it turned me dreamy and contented. After he finished, I lay on my back with Ananias close beside me, and it soon became obvious that he wasn't finished at all. Truth be told, neither was I.

"Were we still back in England," I asked, "conducting ourselves as we both did then, do you think we would have become lovers?"

"I was planning my campaign," he said. "Would I have been successful?"

"Probably," I said. "Given who we both were then."

"And here?"

"Here," I said, as I again took him in my hand, "we are in a new world."

He pushed my hand away and rolled on top of me.

"Ananias, no," I said. He stopped, still on top of me. "That isn't the way," I said.

He closed his eyes, took a long breath, and rolled back off.

"This is," I said, as I rolled on top of him.

twenty-nine

Ananias and I awoke again just as first light was beginning to show. The storm had passed and no longer could we hear thunder or see lightning. I stood and felt my dress where it hung near the long-extinguished fire. It was nearly dry. I put it back on and walked outside. Soon, Ananias followed. He came up behind me as I looked across the water toward the darkened mainland.

"Last night was a terrible mistake," I said.

He put his arms around me and pulled me against him. "Last night was inevitable."

"No, it was not. We should not have let it happen."

He put his lips on the back of my neck. I started to pull away as something on the far shore caught my eye. It looked like a bit of the rising sun, obscured by trees. But the sun did not rise in that direction; it set.

"Look," I said. "Is that a fire?"

It was. And as we stared, several more made themselves apparent.

"Wanchese!" said an urgent voice behind us. Manteo's two men had come out of the woods. One of them pointed at the distant fires and said it again: "Wanchese!"

"We must go," said Ananias. "The colony must be alerted."

"Yes," I agreed. "Go."

"You must come, too, Emme. You cannot stay here outside the palisade."

"No." I shook my head. "I cannot go back until Manteo accompanies me. You know that." He wanted to argue, it was plain to see, but he also needed to make haste. "Go!" I insisted. "I will be safe here."

For only another moment he hesitated, then decided. He kissed me quickly and departed, running down the trail in the half-light. When he had disappeared, I turned to the two Indians. The one who had spoken pointed to the hut and waved, urging me to go back inside.

"Manteo!" he said. He motioned toward Croatoan to the south, then indicated movement toward here. "Manteo," he said again, this time pointing at the ground between us.

That was clear enough: He wanted me to remain inside the hut until Manteo came back. I nodded and went back inside, where I busied myself making a breakfast of dried fish and fruits, then rolling the mats and tidying up. The sun had not yet risen and it was still dark inside the hut, but I made do. By now, I knew where everything was supposed to be.

A grunt came from just outside the hut, followed by sounds of a brief scuffle. I rushed to the entrance and saw an Indian on the ground in front of me. Others crouched farther away, pointing their bows and arrows at me. A single voice shouted something in their language.

"Woman!" the same voice then called. "Come out farther! Now!"

I was too terrified to move. The Indian on the ground by my feet was one of Manteo's men, with arrows protruding from his body. He appeared to be dead. The other one of Manteo's men lay on the ground farther away, in a pool of blood so large I could see it from where I stood.

"Now, woman," shouted the commanding voice. "Come out toward us!" He spoke English the way Manteo did.

I stepped forward, so light-headed with shock and fear that I was barely able to keep my balance. Strong hands suddenly gripped me by both arms from behind, then lifted me up and carried me away from the hut. I was put back down among the crouching Indians in front of one who stood behind them.

"Who else is inside?" he demanded. This had to be Wanchese himself.

"N–No one," I stammered.

"No? Where is Manteo?"

"Not here," I said.

The Indian waved at his men and several rushed inside the hut. They returned waving their arms. The Indian said something to the men holding me, and they let me go.

"You know who I am," he said.

I nodded. "Wanchese."

He nodded. "I am. Who are you?"

"Emme Merrimoth."

"Why are you here, Emme Merrimoth? Has Manteo taken an English wife?"

"No, I am not Manteo's wife."

Wanchese was as tall as Manteo and every bit as imposing. He wore an animal skin breechcloth and a small sheet of copper-colored metal in the center of his chest, hung by a leather string around his neck. His body was covered in intricately applied ornamentation, with prominent circles painted around his nipples and navel. His head was shaved on the sides and his long black hair hung down the back of his neck where three feathers were woven into it. He carried a bow. Tied to his waist was a cylindrical quiver filled with arrows.

The others were similarly clad, though only Wanchese had a metal shield on his chest. Their body paint was not nearly so grand as his, and some of them carried clubs, spears, and wooden swords instead of bows. There were twenty or more of them.

Wanchese squinted his eyes as he thought. "Take off your dress," he said.

My heart thumped in fear. Tears came to my eyes. I shook my head.

"Do as you are told, woman!"

Having little choice, I did. When my dress was off, Wanchese said something to one of his men, who picked it up and took it into the hut, then returned empty-handed. Wanchese said something to another Indian, who ran down toward the beach. He came running back not long after with a small earthen jug and handed it to Wanchese. Wanchese opened it and dipped his finger inside. It came out dripping red dye.

"Turn around," he said. He then traced something on my back with the dye, dipping back into the jug several times.

"Turn around again."

He painted a design on my chest, just below my neck. It was an "X" with three short lines beside it. He then handed the jug to an Indian, who put it inside the hut.

"Manteo and your fellow English will now know that you have been taken," Wanchese said. "They will know that you are marked."

He issued a series of sharp commands. His Indians all started toward the beach where their canoes waited.

"Come, Emme Merrimoth," said Wanchese. "You now belong to me."

thirty

Wanchese and his men took me to Dasamonquepeuk, where burned the fires that Ananias and I had seen at first light. I was made to sit naked with my painted captors in one of their long dugout canoes while the raiding party paddled back across the five miles of open water to the town, the same one that our men had mistakenly attacked after the killing of George Howe. The crossing took almost an hour and I was so numb with fear the entire time that I had trouble breathing. I couldn't help but imagine what might happen to me once we reached the other side.

At the far shore, the Indians paddling the canoes guided them through narrow channels in the high saltwater grasses until we came to a landing place, where we were met by more of Wanchese's people, men, women, and children. All were astonished to see me. As Wanchese guided me from the landing place to the town, he had to repeatedly order them to make room. They all wanted to get closer, to see and even to touch me. The adults obeyed Wanchese, but some of the children did not—they rushed forward to put their small hands on me, only to be pulled back by their mothers. Wanchese had to keep his strong grip on my arm just to hold me up, as I stumbled along the path, more exposed than the Indians who surrounded me.

The town itself was much like Benginoor and Manteo's on Croatoan, but larger. Surrounded by cleared planting fields and grapevines, it had no palisade, and the many houses and huts were arrayed around a large communal fire pit. There were many more people, and it seemed that every one of them had gathered to see me. I realized that I must have been the first English person most of them had ever seen.

In the center of the town, Wanchese made everyone stop and listen to him. He gave what appeared to be a very stern lecture, repeatedly pointing to me while he spoke. After his speech, almost everyone dispersed and began packing things up.

Two older women, perhaps in their forties, came forward and led me to one of the larger houses and took me inside. Both kept touching my skin. One of them rubbed my arm, as if trying to scrape off whatever made my skin color different from theirs. But what really made their eyes widen was my long blond hair. Theirs was black, like the others in their town, and they spat on their hands and then vigorously rubbed my locks, again trying to remove whatever it was that made it so light. It wasn't long before my hair was entirely tangled.

The two women pulled my hair back behind my head and tied it there with a leather string, letting it hang in a long tail. While I stood shaking with fear, they tied one of their deerskin aprons around my waist. Dyed green and fringed with loose threads, it covered only my front from my waist to my knees, leaving me completely bare everywhere else, the same as they were. When they were finished, they took me back outside.

The whole town was a flurry of activity. Families were gathering their baskets, mats, and pottery and carrying them toward the shore, where the boats were beached. Others were leaving the town on foot in an irregular stream of people, all walking in the same direction, away from the shore and toward a beaten path in the forest. One of the two women stayed with me while the other hurried off. She must have returned with instructions, as I was then escorted back to the tall grasses of the shoreline.

Most of the long boats were packed with baskets and earthen containers of all sizes. Some were already being paddled away, with two men in each boat. I was led to one of the waiting boats, in which a small space had been left among the cargo for me to sit. I climbed in and was paddled away by two men, still wearing the painted designs of the ones who had kidnapped me.

For the rest of the day, we traveled. The canoes stayed close together, hugging the shoreline and keeping it on our left side. I took that to mean that we were traveling north, but late in the day, the sun began to sink directly in front of us, which meant we had, at some point, turned to the west. When the sun finally did set, it was more to our right. We had turned toward the south, making our way up an inlet narrow enough that one could see both sides, both of which were lined with a thick forest of tall trees. No one spoke. All I could hear were the slap of the paddles in the water, the calls of strange birds from the forest, and my own breathing. It seemed more dream than reality.

Toward dark, we finally stopped at another town, this one on the right bank of the inlet. It, too, was under Wanchese's control. As our canoe pulled into the landing, I could see that some of the boats that had preceded us had unloaded their cargoes and these boats were now being used to ferry people across the inlet from the far shore. Those people were the ones who had taken the overland path from Dasamonquepeuk.

Once again, I was taken out of the canoe and into the town, joining the line of walkers who had just been ferried across. Inside the palisade, I was ushered to the largest of the ten or twelve houses and taken inside. The house had more than one room, though I could not tell how many, separated from each other by the same kind of woven mats that formed the outside walls, all hung from a frame of thin, bent tree trunks that formed an arched ceiling ten or twelve feet high.

This was the largest room—that much I could tell—and a fire was burning in the center of it. Wanchese awaited me there. With him were five women closer to my age, some children, and a half dozen men whom I took to be his *weroances*. Most were older than Wanchese. All in the room sat, save Wanchese himself.

"Go there," said Wanchese, and pointed to where the other women sat. None of them was smiling. One patted the ground beside herself and I sat there on the well-worn dirt floor.

Wanchese and the elders commenced a long, heated discussion, much of which I ascertained was about me, as each gestured to me as he spoke. Whenever Wanchese agreed with what one of the others had just said, the man would nod and sit up straighter. When Wanchese disagreed, the other man's shoulders slumped and he looked down. While this debate went on, the five women leaned close to one another and whispered, often looking at me. Sometimes they nodded, sometimes they shook their heads. Never did they smile. All I could do was sit and tremble with apprehension.

Eventually, the question was apparently decided. The men rose to their feet and all but Wanchese left. The women and children then stood, too. I started to do the same, but was pushed back down by one of the women nearest me. I sat and watched as two of the women and all of the children went into the back rooms, while the remaining three women set about preparing the evening meal. Two of them rolled out mats and the third fetched a large clay container the size of a large stew pot. It had a pointed bottom. She set it in the center of the burning coals of the fire and held it there while one of the other women placed rocks around its base to prop it up, pulling her hands back quickly to keep from getting burned. The final woman then poured water from another jug into the stabilized cooking pot.

As the water heated toward a boil, the three women cut vegetables and meat into bite-sized pieces, using what appeared to be sharpened mussel shells as their knives. They dropped the chopped meat and vegetables into the broth along with what appeared to be crushed walnuts. In a very short time, it turned into a pleasant-smelling stew, the aromatic steam rising with the fire smoke toward the high ceiling to dissipate. By the time the stew was done, the only light in the whole house was from the central cooking fire, a flickering orange glow that cast dark, dancing shadows on the walls whenever anyone moved about the room.

The two other women and the children came back into the main room and after waiting for Wanchese to do so first, they all sat around the mats. Each had a wooden bowl, which they dipped into the stew for their individual shares. They then ate the cut pieces with their bare hands and drank the broth by tipping the bowls to their mouths. The one who had pushed me back down now waved at me to come and join them. I did, but with little appetite.

As I looked at their firelit faces, sitting together and eating, I realized that this must be Wanchese's family, his five wives and children. Until then, it had not occurred to me that an Indian man might have more than one wife. Was that normal, or just reserved for a chief like Wanchese? Was it true of Manteo's people? If so, how did his mother become the *weroanza*?

For the whole meal, eaten largely in silence, Wanchese's wives stole glances at me, then looked back to Wanchese. Jealousy is universal, and I could see it in their eyes even through my own fear-shrouded gaze in this alien place. I grew more apprehensive about what was to happen after supper. Was I now one of his wives?

When he finished eating, Wanchese stood up. The others did, as well, and I did, too. The women looked back and forth between Wanchese and me. Wanchese then beckoned to one of the women and she went to his side. He said something to the others that made them laugh. He and the chosen one started toward the back rooms. He stopped and looked back at me.

"I have been to your country," Wanchese said. "Englishwomen hold no attraction for me."

The mood of his wives brightened, and they chattered happily as they picked up after the meal. I sat back down. When their work was finished, two of the women repaired to the back of the house with the children. The two who remained rolled out sleeping mats for themselves and for me, motioning that I was to take the one in the middle, and I lay down where I was told. My breasts had started to hurt again, but that discomfort was minor compared to the headache, nausea, and fear that had been with me all day, inner turmoil that had only grown worse as the finality of my situation now set its heavy hand on my entire being.

Outside the house, people began to chant in the dark. The two women on either side of me quietly joined in. From the back of the mat-walled house, other voices joined in, children included, the chanting not quite overpowering the sound of Wanchese making love to one of his wives.

I was lost. In every way I could imagine, my world had come to an end.

thirty-one

At first light the next day, I was taken back to the dugout boats. Wanchese brought me from his house down to the shore, where three boats were being readied by several of his warriors. Four of the elders who had been part of the discussion in Wanchese's house the night before stood on the shore waiting, while the younger men carried baskets and rolled-up sleeping mats to stow in the boats. None of them wore any of the garish paints they had worn the day before and there was no sign of anyone else leaving. Whatever had been decided last night about me, this had to be its result. Was I being taken back to Roanoke? While the optimist in me longed for that, the realist knew it would be better not to think about it at all, which is what I tried to do.

Once the boats were loaded and the younger men had pushed them out into the water, we all waded out to our knees before climbing in. The water was warmer than the night-cooled air. There was no wind. Wanchese and I boarded one of the boats with two paddlers. A thin fog misted the inlet and morning dew dripped from the moss hanging from the shoreline trees. Birdsong filled the air. Waterbirds swam nearby as we quietly paddled away. No one spoke.

After an hour of paddling, we came to the broad bay at the mouth of the inlet. I held my breath. We turned left, toward the west and away from Roanoke. My heart sank. I was to be taken somewhere else.

We paddled north under a warm sun with little or no breeze, keeping close to the marshes and thick forest of the left shore. The other side of the bay was so far that most of the time it could not even be seen. Late in the afternoon, when we came to a place where the bay was not so wide, we crossed. There were fish traps close to the shore, with several canoes moving among them in the shallow water. One of them approached our lead canoe and there was a conversation; then the men in the other canoe turned back toward shore. We could not hear what was being said among the other Indians, nor make out the details of who was in the other canoe. We waited in our three boats for almost an hour, when the Indians in the other canoe finally came back and had another conversation with our men. One of the elders spoke briefly to Wanchese, and then we continued on.

Toward dark, we came to a further narrowing of the bay. Our paddlers steered us to a narrow beach and we landed for the night. Wanchese and the elders paced back and forth, deep in conversation, while the younger men gathered dry wood and made a fire. My skin had begun to feel as if it were burning up, and even in the fading light, I could see that it had turned bright red. It felt as if boiling water were slowly being poured all over me. I had heard about sunburn, but had never suffered from it.

I walked back to the water, intending to slip in for the cooling relief it might afford me. Before I waded out, I scooped a cupped handful and tasted it—it was fresh, which I hoped wouldn't exacerbate my burns. This also told me that we weren't traveling up an inlet, but a great river. Relieved, I took off my deerskin apron, set it on the dry ground, and walked out into the water. It felt wonderful.

"Woman!" shouted Wanchese. "Come back!" He and several of his men started in my direction.

"I'm not going anywhere!" I answered as they came splashing out to me. Wanchese grabbed my arm and I yelled out in pain.

He let go and peered at my skin, squinting in the near dark. The elders came over and one of them looked closely at me, then said something to Wanchese. Wanchese nodded and gave an order to one of the young men, who ran off.

"He says you have the sun cook that white people get." The elder nodded at me as Wanchese translated. "He says to cover it with bear grease and in three days it will go away. Come."

Three days? I wasn't sure I could stand it. I splashed out of the river and walked with the Indians to the campfire. The young man returned with a heavy deerskin pouch. Wanchese gave another order and two of the younger men dipped their hands in the pouch. They pulled out gobs of grease that looked like lard and had very little odor, then stood in front and in back of me and began to spread it onto my skin, starting at my neck and working down. It hurt so much that I almost cried out. But as their hands moved down my body, the burning pain subsided in their wake. The relief was so great that I did not protest even as they applied the salve to every part of me that had been exposed to the sun, eventually working down my legs and finishing with the tops of my feet. By then, I was beginning to feel faint. Few men had ever touched me so thoroughly, and never two at the same time.

When they were finished, one of the two Indians handed me my deerskin apron. They both walked away as indifferent to where their hands had just been as if they had just finished grooming an animal. As I tied the apron back on, it occurred to me that Wanchese's lack of interest in Englishwomen might not just be because he had been to England, as he had said to me. Maybe I was unattractive to all of them. But if not for the reasons I'd feared, why were they going to all this trouble to keep and care for me? I had no answer.

I wish I could say that the bear grease worked magic that night, but it did not. The burning pain returned within the hour. Lying on the woven mat that night was excruciating and I slept not at all.

But the next day, before we started traveling again, the men rigged an awning for me in the boat, lashing cut sticks together and tying a sleeping mat to them just above my head. The shade was welcome, even though the pain continued.

I remember little of the next two days, save the fact that we continued traveling upriver, paddling from dawn to dark and spending the nights along the shore. I have a hazy recollection of our stopping to converse with some Indians from another town on the way, but I cannot for certain say so. I realize now that I must have been suffering from a fever in addition to the heat and pain from my burned skin.

We reached our destination on the fourth day of travel and by then, as the elder had predicted, I was feeling much better. My burned skin was beginning to peel away, but the pain was gone and my mind had returned from wherever it had gone. Only then, as we paddled toward a steep, sandy shoreline on top of which sat what looked to be the largest Indian town I had yet seen, did I wonder how it was that the elder had known anything about "the sun cook that white people get." Where had he learned that?

I was about to discover the answer.

thirty—two

The Indian town sat high upon the outside bank at a great bend in
the river. As our three canoes approached it from downriver, I could
see dozens of houses arrayed along the top of a steep, sandy bank.
People gathered at the edge to look at us, and others hurried down
several angled pathways to the long beach, upon which lay twenty
or more dugout canoes like ours. Some of the boats were being hurriedly pushed into the water while others were already paddling out
to us. By the time we got close to the beach we were surrounded on
land and on water. Remaining just offshore, we stayed in our boats.

Eventually, a delegation of *weroances* and elders came down
the angled path to the beach. Everyone made deferential room
for the six men, and even the canoes cleared a path for our three
canoes to be paddled to the beach in front of the delegation. Wanchese and our four elders went ashore and greeted the six men from
the town. After a brief discussion, Wanchese waved to the paddlers
in my canoe, who then helped me out of the boat and escorted me

to where the senior men stood. As a group, we then walked up the path to the town.

When we reached the top, I was amazed at the size of the Indian town spread out before me. Though I did not know it then, this was Chowanoak, the principal town of the most powerful Indian people in the area. I could not see its edges. It was many times the size of the three Indian towns I had already seen—a city, by comparison. It had no palisade, and instead of one main road down the center, there were several dusty avenues lined with houses of the same sizes and shapes as the ones I had seen before. Even in the midday sun, smoke from interior fires rose from many of the homes. As far as the eye could see, there were no trees, just houses. Its population must have been in the hundreds, if not thousands. I never heard an actual count, but on that first day as I was led into the center of Chowanoak, there certainly were large crowds of people gathering to look at me.

We and the six Chowanoak elders worked our way through the chattering people to the center of the town. There stood a great house, the largest Indian structure I had yet seen. It had the height of a three-story building and the outside wall was the size of an English village church. It seemed to be a permanent structure, for its roof was made of carefully laid tree bark, not woven mats, and its supporting frame was constructed of full-sized tree trunks, not the saplings of the houses I had previously been in. The main entranceway was ten feet tall by as many wide. As we approached it, the Chowanoak elders stepped aside and motioned to Wanchese that he should go inside first. He did, taking me with him, grasping my upper arm and walking swiftly. The elders followed.

"This is the house of Menatonan," he said to me. "A great chief. You are my gift to him."

We entered the main room and there Menatonan himself waited, along with two dozen or so of his attendants. He sat on a raised platform, set back on the right-hand side. Beside him stood a lad of perhaps thirteen or fourteen. The other attendants, adult men and women of varying ages, sat on the benches that lined the walls. A fire burned in the center of the room, but it was so large that there was plenty of space surrounding it in which to move about.

Menatonan himself was unmistakably regal. Upon his head was a crown of gleaming yellow metal adorned with pearls and large feathers of many colors, all of them sticking upward. Over his shoulders draped a lustrous robe of red-dyed deerskin trimmed with black fur. Around his neck he wore several chains of the same shining metal as his crown. But as Wanchese and I approached him, passing between the fire in the center and the seated attendants on their bench on the right, I could see that he was not physically firm. His legs were withered and bent, his shoulders and arms were thin, and his creased and skinny neck seemed barely strong enough to support his large head and the weighty crown atop it. I could not guess at his age. His eyes were bright and he had all his teeth, but his visage was wrinkled as an older man's. When he spoke, I could barely hear him.

My instinct as we came before him was to curtsy, the first time that notion had occurred to me. Not even Manteo's mother had elicited such a response in me. But perhaps the comparison is unfair—here I was a prisoner, and in Benginoor's town I was not. In any case, Wanchese did not bow, nor did he give any other sign of obeisance, so neither did I. I stood before Menatonan, trembling from head to foot.

Wanchese made a short speech. Menatonan nodded gravely and answered with a short discourse of his own. He then turned and spoke directly to me in his language. When he finished, the lad beside him stepped forward.

"My father says that we have been expecting you," said the boy. "He wishes to know your name."

I was struck speechless. The boy spoke perfect English, much better than either Manteo or Wanchese, and with an entirely different accent. The boy looked at me without expression, waiting for an answer, but his father smiled. Menatonan said something to the boy.

"My father says you are surprised to hear me speaking English."

150

I glanced at Menatonan, then at Wanchese. If he, too, was surprised, he kept it hidden. I looked back at the boy. "Emme," I managed. "Emme Merrimoth."

Menatonan spoke again to the boy, and I caught my name in the middle of what he said.

"We thank the great chief Wanchese for his most generous gift of Emme Merrimoth," translated the boy. "We welcome you to Chowanoak, Emme Merrimoth. Come and stand beside me."

The boy beckoned for me to come forward and stand with him next to Menatonan. I did, my heart racing. Menatonan spoke directly to Wanchese, who answered in their language and then turned abruptly and left. His four elders followed him outside. When they were gone, Menatonan feebly raised his right arm. It shook with weakness, but its effect was instant—the attendants who had been sitting and watching stood up and quickly filed out the front door. Only the boy and I remained with Menatonan.

"Sit," said Menatonan in very accented English. "Front."

Following the boy's lead, I sat on the ground beside him, both of us facing the great chief.

"Tell," he said to the boy, who nodded and turned to me.

"My father is learning English. He does not yet speak it well. He does not want his people to hear him speak in any way that does not carry great authority. Therefore, he will not speak English in front of them. Is this understood?"

My head was swimming. How could any of this not be a dream? I nodded. "Yes," I said. The boy turned back to his father and so did I.

"You here," said Menatonan. "You English with me. You English with him. Yes?"

His English was much more like Manteo's and Wanchese's than his son's, singsong and disconcerting. Again, I nodded. "Yes," I answered.

"You questions, him answer. Yes?"

"Yes."

"Good. Go."

He waved his withered arm as he had before and the boy jumped to his feet. I stood, too, and the boy took my elbow and led me toward the back of the house. Several women hurried back in the direction from which we had just come.

"My father's servants," said the boy. "He is never alone."

He took me down a long, narrow corridor of hung mats. Shards of sunlight streamed through the gaps in the walls and the smell of woodsmoke lingered in every space. We went into a small room at the back of the great house. The floor was covered with mats and the boy motioned for me to sit with him.

"My name is Skiko," he said. "I am my father's oldest son." He looked at me as if he expected me to say something. When I did not, he continued.

"Two years ago, I was taken prisoner by Ralph Lane and held by him for many months before he returned me here to my father. Have you heard that story?"

I shook my head. "No."

"I am surprised," he said. "Do you know of him? Has he come back again?"

"No, he has not come back again. I know him only by name."

"I see."

"Is that where you learned English?"

"Some of it. Why? Do I not speak it well?"

"You speak it very well. Better than Wanchese or Manteo."

"Manteo!" Skiko exclaimed. "Do you know Manteo? Has he come back?"

"Yes, he has. He is now our governor."

Skiko's eyes went wide. "Manteo is your governor? Not an Englishman?"

"Yes. He was appointed by an agent of our queen."

He stood up. "Come," he said. "My father must hear of this immediately."

Together we hurried back through the house to the great room where Menatonan still sat on his platform. His attendants busied themselves nearby. In a rapid burst of their language, Skiko spoke to his father. While he listened, Menatonan kept glancing at me. When his son stopped, the old man closed his eyes. His head canted left and then right, and I thought I saw his lips barely moving, as if he were reciting a prayer to himself. Eventually, he opened his eyes again and looked at me.

"You," he said. "Manteo. Tell true?"

"Yes," I answered. "I am telling the truth. Manteo is our governor."

He stared intently into my eyes. He nodded. "Yes. You tell true."

He turned to Skiko and spoke several long sentences to him, then lifted his arm in the signal I now knew. I followed Skiko out of the great room and again into the back corridor.

"Come," he said as we continued past the small room we had been in before. "My father has given instructions."

Skiko took me out the back door of the great house and into the midday sunshine. Keeping his hand on my elbow, he guided me through a maze of well-worn, dusty lanes, and the children and adults working and playing among the rows of their houses looked up curiously as we passed. Women ground corn with mortar and pestle; others wove mats or carried baskets of food or seashells. Men chinked at bits of stone or shell, and then their companions fastened the chinked cutting edges to wooden handles or cut wood with finished versions of the same tools. Only the smallest children played, as the adolescents worked alongside the adults, girls with women, boys with men.

After several disorienting turns through the town, Skiko brought me to a sturdy-looking house set apart from the others. It was entirely covered with tree bark and it was guarded. Two imposing Indians stood blocking the open doorway, one with a sharp wooden sword in his hand and another with a thick-handled axe. Skiko said something to them and they stepped aside to let us pass.

Inside, it was darker than it would be in a mat-sided house, and it took a moment for my eyes to adjust. There was no fire. Four long, narrow tables were set in a square around the center of the single room, a neat stack of closed baskets in the center of the square. Seated around the outside of the tables were ten or twelve women, each of them hunched over their work on the section of the table in front of them. While they worked, two men paced about the inside of the square, checking the women's work. As my eyes became accustomed to the gloom, I could see that there was something different about the two supervisors—they both had full, dark beards.

"Anthony and William," Skiko said. "Come here."

They were Englishmen! As undressed as any Indian, to be sure, but Englishmen, no doubt. They looked up and were just as astonished to see me. Both ducked under the table and rushed over to us.

"Do not speak!" commanded Skiko.

Like a pair of barely restrained mastiffs, the two men held themselves in check.

"The English have returned to Roanoke," said Skiko. "This time they have brought women and children. This woman was among them. Like you, she now belongs to us."

The two glanced at each other, then back at me. Their shoulder-length brown hair and heavy beards were stringy and matted. Their deerskin aprons were tattered and ripped, their chests smeared with grime, their fingernails black with dirt. There were jagged scars on their arms and faces—some old, some fresh—and their eyes were wild as they roved all over me. I had finally grown accustomed to being without clothes among the indifferent Indians, but now I was naked again.

"You will be allowed to speak with her later," said Skiko. "Now return to your house and make yourselves presentable. My father has commanded your presence immediately."

They both continued staring at me. The one on the right opened his mouth.

"Do *not* speak!" shouted Skiko. "Do as you are told!"

His raised voice brought the two armed warriors into the building. The Englishmen glared at them. Skiko said something to the guards, who then escorted the Englishmen out the door. When they were gone, Skiko led me back outside. The men had turned left; we went right, walking swiftly.

"They have become less civilized since my father made slaves of them," said Skiko. "It is a shame, for they were once my friends."

"Where did they come from?" I asked.

"They were with Governor Lane."

"How did they get here?"

"It is a story for another time. Now I will take you to the other one."

"There is another one?"

"Yes. We are going to collect him now."

At the edge of the town, we walked at a rapid pace past fields of harvested corn and still-growing melons, then through a shaded patch of forest and toward a small cleared field, where perhaps a dozen young men were gathered. Two of them were fighting with their wooden swords while the others watched and shouted encouragement. In addition to the short wooden sword, in his other hand each man held a small wooden knife.

As we came closer, one of those watching turned and saw us. He said something and the other watchers turned to stare, too. Only the two fighters continued as before, unaware of us as they flailed at each other, thrusting and parrying, sharp *thwacks* sounding as their swords struck each other. As Skiko brought me closer to the two dark-skinned fighters, it took me a moment to resolve what it was about the scene that seemed odd. And then I had it: One of them had long blond hair. Like mine, it was tied back in a tail.

"Richard!" shouted Skiko.

"What?" answered the blond fighter without looking at Skiko.

Skiko called the man's name again. Again, the blond fighter answered, though more irritated this time, "What?" He glanced our way.

He had blue eyes—another Englishman. He froze when he saw me. Unfortunately, the Indian fighter did not, and smote him so harshly on his shoulder that it knocked him down. The Englishman jumped back to his feet and held up his hand to his opponent. He did not take his eyes off me as he came over to us. Like his opponent, he wore only a loincloth and a full sheen of dripping sweat, under which lay the darkest skin I had ever seen on an Englishman. His entire body was the color of a sailor's hands and face. He also was clean-shaven, like the Indians.

He stopped directly in front of me, still breathing hard from the exertion of his fighting.

"Richard Poore," said Skiko, "this is Emme Merrimoth."

Richard took a half step back and bowed. "At your service, madam," he said with a smile. "The pleasure is mine."

"And yours alone, sir," I said. "I find no pleasure in any of this."

Skiko interrupted our greeting. "My father has commanded us all to come before him immediately. We must hurry."

Richard turned to the other Indians and said something to them in their language, apparently ending the fighting, for they seemed disappointed and began gathering their swords and knives. The three of us then began walking swiftly back toward the town, Skiko on one side of me and Richard Poore on the other.

"So," said Richard as we walked, "to what do we owe this gift of providence? Are you shipwrecked? Please do not tell me that some fool in England has sent proper women to this Inquisitor's dungeon they call the new world."

"Do I look a proper woman to you, sir? Because I certainly do not feel one at the moment."

"Point taken, madam. Could I do so, I would avert my eyes. But I cannot."

"Clearly," I said. "To answer your question, I have come with a colony from London. We are established at Roanoke Island."

"Led by whom? Lane? Grenville? Raleigh himself?"

"John White."

"John White, the artist? A governor?"

"Yes, but he has already left and gone back to England. Ananias Dare now acts in his place."

"I know him not. How many are you?"

"One hundred seventeen."

"Including women?" he asked.

"And children."

He rolled his eyes. "A fool's errand, doomed already. How came you here?"

"I was captured by Wanchese. He brought me here."

Richard's eyes flew wide in surprise. He looked past me to Skiko. "Wanchese was here? Why was I not told?"

"My father did not want you to know."

Richard nodded. "That would be true."

"There is more," said Skiko. "Manteo has returned."

Richard looked at me with great surprise. "Manteo? 'Tis true?"

"Yes. He is our governor."

"What?"

"True enough. Appointed by Her Majesty by written decree."

"The world has upended itself," Richard said. "Does Wanchese know of it?"

"He knows Manteo is back. He was trying to kill him when I was taken."

Richard nodded to himself. "And so it starts."

In Menatonan's great house, the other two Englishmen had already arrived, scrubbed clean and seated along the benches with a gathering of very serious-looking *weroances* and elders. As we entered the room, the ones sitting closest to the platform made room for the three of us. I sat between Skiko and Richard, arranged as we had been on our walk.

The meeting began with a speech by Menatonan. As he spoke, Richard leaned over to whisper his hurried translation into my ear.

"Wanchese has told us the English are back . . . as you know, he brought this woman as proof . . . He has asked us to join him in war against the English . . . But there is something Wanchese did not tell us . . . He's now talking about you . . . She says Manteo is back . . . He is chief of the English—"

At that point a wave of astonishment swept over the assembled. Several people shouted. Richard continued, "They disbelieve. They want proof . . ." He seemed suddenly anxious.

"What?" I whispered.

"You are about to be questioned directly."

At an order from his father, Skiko brought me to stand before the gathered senior men. One of the elders stood and asked a question. He kept pointing at me. Skiko translated: "Are we to believe a woman? Wanchese himself was just here and said nothing about Manteo. Tell us your proof, Englishwoman."

I looked at Skiko. He nodded. "Tell it," he said.

But what proof did I have beyond my own word? I could think of nothing to say. "You must answer," said Skiko. I took a breath to calm myself.

"I have no proof," I said. Skiko translated. The elder nodded and waved his arm in triumph. "But I am telling the truth," I went on. At Skiko's translation, the elder who had questioned me laughed. A few laughed with him.

The elder then made a speech of his own, which Skiko translated for me. "We have no reason to believe her," he said. "The English are our enemies. They lie, as we all have learned. She lies, too. If Manteo has come back, Wanchese would have told us so. He did not." Many of the elders and *weroances* agreed, as even I could tell.

"I traveled across the ocean with Manteo," I said, unable to keep quiet. "I was at the ceremony when he was made governor. I have been to his town on Croatoan."

Skiko translated, and my words resulted in renewed discussion. The disbelieving elder, through Skiko's translation, asked me, "Who is the chief there? Is it Manteo?"

"No," I answered. "It is his mother. Her name is Benginoor. She came to Roanoke to witness the ceremony."

The reaction was immediate from the elders and *weroances*. Menatonan raised his arm and the room went instantly silent. He canted his head and Skiko led me back to my seat.

"Well parried," Richard whispered in my ear as Menatonan spoke. "You have them guessing now."

158

The chief ordered a delegation be sent to Croatoan to see for themselves whether or not Manteo was there, and whether or not he had been named governor of the English.

Richard shook his head. "It won't work," he whispered.

"Why not?" I whispered back.

"Wanchese will not let it happen. He is not strong enough to attack the English alone. He needs these Indians as allies. Right now, they are undecided. If Menatonan accepts that Manteo is governor at Roanoke, he will accept the English, not fight them."

Menatonan then lifted his arm, dismissing the gathering. We all stood. As people began to file out of the great room, Menatonan pointed to Richard, Skiko, and me, and beckoned us toward him. We three went and stood before him. The chief then said something to Richard while pointing toward me. Richard answered in their language. Menatonan spoke again, and we were dismissed.

Outside the great house, the three of us walked back the way we had come. Partway there, Skiko abruptly parted company with us, turning left down a narrow lane without saying a word.

"Where is he going?" I asked Richard.

"Anywhere he wants. He is the crown prince."

"Where are we going?"

"To my house. Or, I should say now, our house."

"Our house?"

"Our house. Menatonan has given you to me."

"I am now to be your slave?"

"No. We are both Menatonan's slaves. You are now my wife."

"I am not your wife."

"Yes, you are," he insisted. "Menatonan has decreed it."

It took ten more minutes of walking to reach Richard's house. Neither of us spoke. I know not what was in his mind. Truth be told, I could barely find my own thoughts. Since the morning Wanchese had taken me, the events of my life had come and gone so rapidly, I could hardly grasp any of them. I tried desperately to think of a way to dissuade Richard from what he now intended. I barely had time.

Richard led me into his home. The side mats of his hut were all lowered and it was cooler and darker inside than out. I stood in the center of the room and he went to a basket to fetch something. I tried to stall for more time.

"Who are you, Richard Poore?" I asked

"Richard Poore no longer exists," he said.

"Who were you, then?"

He retrieved a sleeping mat from the basket. He rolled it out on the floor, then came back and stood before me.

"Someone who would not have dreamed this. Let down your hair."

"Do not touch me. I am not your wife. And I am not your slave. I am an Englishwoman and you are an Englishman and that is how we shall behave, even here, among these savages."

"They aren't savages."

"Then why are you acting like one?"

He took a deep breath.

I looked at the sleeping mat. "Do you have another of those?" I asked.

"I can get one," he said.

"Then please do so. You shall sleep on this one and I shall sleep on the other. And I'll not be naked with you. Can you get me something to wear?"

"From where? England? The women here wear naught but what you have on now."

It was my turn to take a deep breath. "Then can you at least pretend that I am clothed?"

"Impossible. Is that not apparent to you?"

It was. "Then go find one of your Indian women. You'll not have me."

"I have no Indian women."

"Then one of your Indian boys."

That was a mistake. His glare was not the only part of him that hardened. He came toward me.

I put up my hands. "I'm sorry. I didn't mean—"

"No more talk." He reached for me.

I backed away and it came to me.

"You cannot do this," I said. "I am betrothed to the governor." He stopped. "If you so much as touch me," I hurriedly continued, "I'll have you hanged."

While he took that in, still visibly inflamed, I pressed my advantage. I knew it was tenuous, at best. "We may be captives now, but not for long. As soon as the governor returns with supplies and reinforcements, we shall surely be freed. And you shall want to remain so, am I not right?"

I watched him deflate and knew I had won. But for how long? We still had to live together in these circumstances. But fences are best mended with the pieces still at hand, so I pressed ahead.

"I know how awkward this is, Richard Poore," I said, "but let us try to make the best of it. If Menatonan has decreed that we be man and wife, then I shall try to be a good wife to you. In every way but that one. What say you? Can we make this bargain together? Can I trust you to keep it?"

He hesitated, apparently collecting his own thoughts. Then he said, "I am not a ravisher of unwilling women. Nor am I a man who breaks his word. We can indeed try to make the best of this, though I will say to you now that it will be far from easy for me. Far, far from it."

thirty-three

And so began the part of my life in the new world that I still think of as a dream, and not a good one. So many of the events came and went the way they do in a nightmare—strange, frightening, and unpredictable. The nightmare continued all through that winter and into the spring. Seven and a half months.

From that first day in Chowanoak, like it or not, I was Richard's Indian wife. I say "Indian," because in every regard, save the color of my skin—and my hair, of course—that's what I became. I kept his house, tended his share of the town's corn and bean fields, cooked his meals, and gave him occasional comfort in the night. Upon this last element I should elaborate. It soon became clear to me that his bodily desire and our nakedness would not remain separated for long in such close confines, so I offered to relieve him in the way I had first offered to Ananias in Manteo's hut. It was infrequent and entirely one-sided. I took no pleasure in it, nor did I in any of my other wifely obligations to Richard.

Neither did the other two English prisoners, Anthony Rottenbury and William Backhouse. As I had already seen, those two were held on a much shorter tether than was Richard. They were treated like slaves, while Richard was treated with deference, more like a gentleman awaiting release upon payment of an expected ransom. It would be some time before I learned the details of why that was so. What I could see right away was that the jealousy of the other two toward Richard burned deeply within them both and grew even hotter after they learned that Menatonan had given me to their rival.

Richard was a great talker. That much was at least bearable, for he had many stories to tell, all of them new to me. Skiko, too, was a storyteller, and the best of the tales I heard were told when he came to our house to share a meal. Those evenings were almost enjoyable, for Skiko and Richard had been on many adventures together and were eager to relate them to me.

The first one they told me was about the capture of Richard and the other two Englishmen. It was, they explained, all the fault of Ralph Lane, the governor of the colony that left here the year before we came.

Lane's colony had arrived two years previous, in the summer of 1585. There were 108 men, including John White and Simon Fernandez. Coming back with them were Manteo and Wanchese, both of whom had been taken to England the year before by the very first English expedition to this part of the new world. They landed at Roanoke and were met by a great chief named Ensenore and his two sons, Wingina and Granganimeo. Those three ruled all the land now controlled by Wanchese, who was one of their young *weroances* before he was taken back to England.

Ensenore was very friendly to the English, as was Granganimeo. They had spent much time with the English during the first expedition in 1584 and had gotten along very well with them. The other son, Wingina, had been recovering from a war wound when the English first arrived and thus remained suspicious.

When Lane and his men began to build their new English village at Roanoke—the one we had just finished repairing—Manteo remained with them, but Wanchese returned to his Indian life. He soon became a confidant of Wingina and convinced the skeptical brother that the English should not be trusted. Soon, he and Wingina were plotting ways to undermine the English colony.

Richard and the other soldiers were tasked with exploring the country while the tradesmen built the village. Led by Governor Ralph Lane and guided by Manteo, a group of forty soldiers, including Richard, left Roanoke and came up these rivers, looking for gold and other treasures. They got as far as the lands of the next great tribe inland, the Mangoaks, who own a great fortune of *wassador*, a mixture of copper and gold that they strain from the River of Death at a place called Chaunis Temoatan. They have so much, said Richard, that they decorate their houses with plates of it. Skiko agreed that this was true.

That upriver expedition took Richard and the others many weeks, and it was this long absence that led Wingina to falsely claim that his warriors had killed them. When they came downriver alive, the myth of the immortal Englishman was created.

All this time, Skiko was living with the English in their new village at Roanoke. Earlier, his father had been captured by Ralph Lane and was only released when he agreed to let the English keep his favorite son as a hostage, to guarantee that Menatonan would remain friendly. Menatonan did, and Skiko was treated well by the English, so well that he learned not only the language, but to like them, too.

Meanwhile Wingina and his allies fought the English. This lasted for many months, long enough for Skiko to gain the freedom to travel to and from Roanoke. During his visits to the other Indian villages Skiko learned of Wingina's latest plot to attack and kill the English. He warned the colonists and they were able to kill Wingina and thwart the plan, which Richard and Skiko both told me would probably have succeeded if not found out.

Governor Lane was now indebted to Skiko and decided to return him to his father in gratitude. He assigned Richard, Anthony, and

William to escort Skiko back upriver to his home at Chowanoak. But while the four were traveling here, a great English fleet arrived off Roanoke unexpectedly. Governor Lane took all of his colonists aboard ships in that fleet and left for England, leaving Skiko's English escorts behind. When the Indians realized this, they took the English soldiers captive. And that's where they had been ever since.

"Why did they make you slaves?" I asked Richard.

"Because that is our way," answered Skiko. "Is it not yours?"

I supposed it was. Again, I wished Audry were here—but not as a slave like me, of course. I wondered what she might be doing right then, after the evening meal in Roanoke, among my own kind, still living our way.

But I soon banished that thought. There is no point in looking out a sunny window if you can never go outside to enjoy it. Better to keep the room dark and try to make the best of it.

thirty-four

Now I really am running out of time to finish this before the council. But I must not cut short the telling of what happened upriver. To me. To Anthony and William. To Skiko. And especially what happened to Richard, God rest him, for now I am with child again—and he is the father.

I cannot say for certain how much of my upriver time was a dream and how much really happened. Certainly I am with child. Certainly Richard is dead, for I saw it happen. I am less certain of all the other details.

But never mind—time is short. All I can do is record what I remember. If some of it be true and some be dream, so be it. It was all real to me.

For the first month or so of my captivity, I was sullen and unhappy. Who would not be? The optimist in me had fallen silent, the seeker of brighter things had gone blind. By day I worked through my chores without a smile, by night I comforted Richard without comment. Eventually even he grew tired of it.

"Were you ever happy, Emme Merrimoth?" he demanded one night. "Back in England, or even in Roanoke? Or have you always been dour and silent?"

"It doesn't matter," I answered.

"Yes," he said. "It does. So tell me. Were you?"

"Dour and silent?" I replied. "No. I was not. I enjoyed being with others, and they with me."

He thought about that for a moment, then stood. "Stand with me," he said. When I had, he asked, "Can you stand still? Very, very still?"

"I suppose so."

"Show me."

I did as he bade. Suddenly, he lunged toward me, and I jumped back, startled.

"You cannot," he said.

"I thought you were going to strike me."

"Stand still anyway. Try it again."

I stood and he lunged again. I only flinched this time. "We will keep doing this," he said. "It will take a few days. But when you do not move at all, you will be ready."

"For what?"

"You will see. It will make you happy, I hope."

For the next two days and nights, whenever we were alone together in his hut, Richard trained me to stand very still no matter what he did to surprise me. Sometimes he would lunge, sometimes he would throw something to the ground, other times he would shout. Eventually, I stopped moving when he did, able to stand as still as Manteo could, though not so long as he did. But Richard didn't want hours, only minutes or seconds. And I could do that.

"You are ready," he said on the third night.

"For what?"

"To take a walk with me. Outside this town."

"We can't do that," I said. "They won't let us."

167

"They won't see us," he said, and moved a storage pot aside to sweep the dirt beneath it, revealing a small wooden door. He lifted the door and retrieved what looked like a pile of black feathers, but I soon saw that the feathers were sewn together into a pair of hooded cloaks. He handed the smaller one to me. The pitch-black feathers were so cleverly stitched together that in an instant we were both enshrouded from head to foot.

"Now," he said, "we are going to walk outside of this town. We are going to move from hut to hut. We are going to remain silent and when I squeeze your arm, you are going to stand motionless, no matter what happens. Because when we stand still in these cloaks, no one will see us."

I nodded.

"One more thing," he said. "When you stand still, look down and squint your eyes. Otherwise they're far from invisible. See?"

He popped his open. I was so nervous I almost laughed.

He smiled. "See? It's working already."

He then led me outside into the dark night. Richard had chosen well—there was no moon, and a layer of clouds obscured even the starlight. One could just make out the silhouettes of the nearby huts and houses as we slipped from one to the next, close enough to hear people rustling and snoring inside them. Periodically, Richard would squeeze my arm and we both would freeze. Whether he actually saw something that made him stop each time or was testing me, I could not tell. My heart was beating so loudly that I was sure someone inside one of the huts would hear it.

Eventually we came to the edge of the town and then into the surrounding forest. "If you hear something," Richard whispered, "be not afraid. It will only be a deer or a bear."

"A bear?" I whispered back.

"Of no consequence. They are afraid of us."

Through the woods we walked, though for how long I do not know. Perhaps a half hour, perhaps more. We came to a hill, with a steep face on one side and, at the bottom of the face, a cave. At first I did not see it, for its opening was obscured by shrubs and small trees. But Richard knew it was there and showed me the way inside.

I could see nothing, of course. It was the darkest of nights and now we were inside a small cave. "Stand right here," he directed. I waited while he stepped away, then rummaged in the dark, struck a flint, and lit a candle.

The cave came alive, and I was struck dumb. We were in an English room, if primitive. There was a table with two chairs, a real bed, and a set of curtains hanging on the cave's wall.

"Where did . . . ? How did—?"

"Skiko got it for me. After my colony abandoned the English fort at Roanoke and left us here, Skiko took some of his father's men to the fort and took some of the things they had left behind. He thought it would make it easier for Anthony, William, and me if we had some English things. But his father said no, it must all be returned to await the next colony, which was sure to come. So Skiko took most of it back, but he kept this furniture. He and I brought it here. And he was right—it has been a great comfort to me, as I hope it will be for you now. No one else knows about it."

"Not Anthony and William?" I asked.

"Especially not them," he said.

We took off our black feather cloaks, as there was nobody to hide from in here. Richard lit another candle while I walked around the small room.

"How often do you come here?" I asked.

"Rarely," he said. "The risk is great. Not even Skiko can guess what his father might do should he find out about it."

"Why did we risk it tonight?"

"Because I wanted you to see it."

He sat down on one of the two chairs. I continued to walk around, running my hands over the English furniture. "It's lovely, Richard," I finally said, and sniffed. "It brings tears to my eyes."

"It did the same to me when Skiko and I first set it up."

"But no longer?"

"Look at me," he said. I did. There were tears in his eyes, too. "The first since then," he continued. "Because now you are here with me. Now it is ours to share."

I turned away. He stood and came up behind me, put his arms around me.

"We can come here as often as you like," he said. "Just the two of us. No one else, ever. It can be our secret home."

"And who will we be when we do that? Richard Poore and Emme Merrimoth? Or two nameless souls who will come here together, dreaming of our real home? The one we shall never see again."

"Oh, we shall see England again, Emme," he said. "Of that I have never had a doubt. The English will keep coming back, and when they next do, they shall find a happily married couple of their own kind, living in a secret English bungalow hidden in the woods, making the best of their temporary lives among the Indians and patiently awaiting their arrival."

"Are we happily married, Richard? Is that what you think we are?"

"I know I am. And I sorely wish you were, too."

How long do thoughts last? How much time passes while your mind resets itself, while the person you have always been suddenly decides on her own to reassert herself? Minutes? Hours? No, certainly not hours. But reassert herself she did, the old Emme Merrimoth, right then and there. Like a dark, compressing weight being lifted and replaced by a warm summer breeze, the optimist in me returned. And in truth, it did seem to happen in an instant.

I pulled away from Richard, turned to look at him. "I'll have a bargain with you, Richard Poore. Take it or leave it."

"I'm listening."

"For as long as we are incarcerated together in that Indian town, you and I shall not be man and wife, no matter what Menatonan decrees or you claim. We shall be what we truly are—slaves taken against our will and forced upon each other. But here, in this secret place, in this make-believe England where we both can dream, you shall have a proper English wife. But only here. In the Indian town, you will no longer be tended to by your fellow slave like an animal—you will no longer be tended to at all. But here, in this place, you and your proper English wife will make love to each other in a civilized and respectful manner. And we shall behave like man and wife. If your proper English wife says she is indisposed, you will restrain yourself that night."

I looked him steadily in the eye. He looked back just as evenly.

"Do we have an arrangement?" I said. He nodded and I smiled. "Now, you will find that your new wife is rarely indisposed, so fear not on that point. But she does have one question."

He raised an eyebrow.

"Is that English bed over there well put together? Is it up to the strain we are about to impose upon it?"

Now he smiled.

thirty-five

I wish I could say that becoming Richard's English wife was as simple and smoothly accomplished as the version of it that I just wrote. The real version—

That word again: *real*. I keep using it here, don't I? But is there an alternative? If I can think of one before I finish this journal you will know it, because I will go back and change it in every case. Or have I already done that? Have you arrived at this page after seeing it scratched out and replaced many times already?

Now there's an unsettling thought—that you may now have a better sense of my reality than I do myself as I write it. Though of course you do. If you are reading this journal, then it has been finished. You can see how long it is; you may even know how it ends. But both are unknown to me in this moment.

Enough of that. There isn't time. I can see it in the sky. The day of the council is already here. I shall return to the story.

The more complete story of how Richard and I grew more comfort-able with each other took many weeks. We could not go to our English cave very often—only on the darkest of nights—so the bulk of our time together was unchanged, as dreary and arduous as it had been before. Still, the bargain was sealed on that initial night of discovery and Richard was true to his word: In the Indian town of Chowanoak we no longer rutted like savages on the ground. In fact, we no longer rutted there at all—though in our English cave, we more than made up for it. In his now-patient hands, I once again found my voice. And I shall leave it at that.

Richard was the best fighter of all the men in our town. He had proven this many times in combats before my arrival, both in real fights with the Mangoaks and with Wanchese's men, and in ritual combat here in Chowanoak, as Richard taught Menatonan's men how to fight English style, with a wooden sword or an axe in one hand and a shield or knife in the other. That's what I had seen him doing on the day Skiko had taken me to meet him.

Anthony and William, I was told, could fight well, too. But Mena-tonan had decided not to trust them. Richard said it was because they had tried too many times to escape. Skiko said it was because they had tried to steal too many things here in town. Both agreed that Mena-tonan's decision was correct.

"Did you not try to escape?" I asked Richard one night after Skiko had left.

"Of course I did," he answered. "Anthony, William, and I did it together. And we succeeded. I led them over land all the way back to the wide water, where we could see Roanoke. We then stole a canoe from some of Wanchese's men and paddled it to the island. But no one was there. The fort was well built but abandoned. There wasn't even food. The Indians had taken it all, along with the hand weapons. Winter was coming. I told the other two that we could not stay there, or anywhere else for that matter, without starving, or being killed by Wanchese's men if we were discovered. There was nothing to be done but to return, to the one band of Indians who might decide to keep us alive until the next set of English arrived."

"And you never tried again?" I asked.

"I did not. The other two did, several times. Finally, Menatonan placed them under guard day and night. I chose a different path to survival, to ally myself with these Indians, to teach them to fight our way so they could hold off Wanchese's attacks from downriver and the Mangoaks from up. I reasoned to myself that when the next English arrived, I might have been able to create a stronger ally for them among the Indians, which they would need in their inevitable confrontation with Wanchese."

Over time, Richard had become a trusted leader of Menatonan's fighters. Even Skiko took his orders in battle. And in the early fall—the days were still hot and the nights not yet very cool—Richard and Skiko were ordered by Menatonan to lead a group of warriors far upriver and over land to the territory of the Mangoaks. The purpose was to spy on the Mangoaks and to try to learn how much of the *wassador* they really had. Menatonan was worried that the Mangoaks might be accumulating so much of it that they could buy allies from other lands, creating an alliance strong enough to attack and seize Chowanoak.

The night before they left, I cooked dinner for them.

"How long will you be gone?" I asked.

"A week, perhaps more," answered Richard. "Not a month."

"Can I come, too?" I asked.

They both laughed. "It's not women's work," said Skiko.

"Why not?" I asked. "I can walk as far as a man. I can see and hear and remember as well as a man. And I can cook. Can any of your men do that?"

"We won't be cooking," said Richard. "A fire might give us away. We bring only men who can fight and eat dried food on the run. Can you do that?"

"But I thought there wouldn't be any fighting," I said. "You're just hiding and looking for *wassador*."

"If all goes well," said Richard, nodding. "But if not . . ."

"If not," Skiko said with a laugh, "your husband will kill all the Mangoaks and then we'll be the ones with all the *wassador*."

We all laughed, but only the two of them did so heartily. It wasn't that I really wanted to go with them. What truly worried me, though I did not say so, was the thought of being left behind with Anthony and William, without my two main protectors nearby. And I had good reason to be afraid: Neither man had stopped leering at me, undisguised lust in their eyes whenever our paths crossed, which they did daily in the fields and gardens on the outskirts of town.

Anthony and William were forced, as part of their slavery, to work in the fields like we women did, and they spent each day running their eyes over me in ways that I can barely describe now without a shudder of revulsion. And it wasn't just their eyes that became aroused at the sight of me—none of us women could miss that. But all we could do was shake our heads in disgust. That female reaction, I'm happy to remember, was common to us all.

I knew I could not safely remain behind. I had to convince them to take me with them.

"Will Anthony and William be going with you?" I asked.

"No," said Skiko. "My father knows that they would only try to run away again."

"So I am to be left here with them?" I asked, this time looking directly at Richard. "Is that what you want?"

Richard started to say something, then stopped. He turned to Skiko. "No," he said, perhaps to me, though he still looked at the lad, "that is not what I want."

For a moment, neither spoke. "I will raise the question with my father," Skiko finally said to Richard. "She is a valuable property. I will want to tell him that you guarantee her safety."

"Tell him that I guarantee it as much as I guarantee the safety of his eldest son," said Richard. "But only if both remain close to me."

thirty-six

There were twelve of us on the *wassador* expedition: nine Indian men, Skiko, Richard, and me. Each member of the party, save me, carried multiple weapons: a bow, a quiver of arrows, a knife of sharpened bone, and either a wooden sword or axe. Richard gave me a knife to carry.

"If our carried rations run out, we will kill meat to eat. You will skin and butcher it."

"I thought we weren't to cook."

"We won't cook it."

"Then I shan't eat it."

He smiled. "Yes, you will, if need be."

We set out at dawn, and for four days we traveled for the entirety of each day's light. Half the time we walked, but the other half we moved faster, at more of a trot. It was plain that the others could easily have kept up the faster pace all day but I needed the slower-paced times to regain my breathing. It was embarrassing. Had I not told Richard and Skiko that I could walk as far as any man?

176

"Please don't slow down for me," I said to Richard after the first several hours on the trail. "I can keep up."

"One," he said, "you cannot. You have not been trained as we have. And two, we would maintain this pace even without you. It preserves our strength, in case we are discovered and must truly run—or stand and fight."

I would be capable of neither, as I well knew. I began to wonder if I had made the wrong decision.

Each night, Richard assigned half of the men to stay awake on guard. The other half of the group slept, for the next night it would be their turn. Before sleep, Richard had us gather branches and tie them together into the shapes of sleeping men. These we laid close together, as if we were all asleep on the ground, and those who did sleep found places nearby to hide and keep watch. Those on guard were each stationed near a sleeping man. I, of course, was not assigned to keep watch overnight. While I slept, either Richard or Skiko stood guard near to me.

Should we suffer a night attack, Richard's orders were to let any approaching Mangoaks pass by on their way into our false camp and then to awaken the sleeping men. The Mangoaks would want to strike at our sleeping bodies at the same time, so they would all rush upon the bundles of sticks at once. Our men would then attack the Mangoaks from all sides.

Hearing this, as you can easily guess, I did not sleep well. Some nights, in fact, I slept not at all, for the forest creatures do not, either. They make frightening noises, especially the bears, which sound much like a man moving cautiously through the darkened shrubs. The first time I heard one, Richard was on guard beside me.

"What is that?" I whispered to him. "Are we being attacked?"

"A bear," he answered sharply, just loud enough to send it crashing away. "Had it been a Mangoak, you would have just killed us all. Next time you are afraid, hold your tongue and reach out to touch me instead."

Chastened, I tried to sleep, but, of course, could not. I had imposed myself upon these men out of fear for my own safety, and now not only was I in even greater peril, but I was threatening their safety, as well.

The next day, we resumed our rapid journey toward the Mangoaks. If any of the Indians held animosity toward me, none of them showed it. In fact, they appeared so habitually even-tempered and stoic, they rarely showed any emotion at all on the journey.

In the new world forests, there are no trails. But Richard and the Indians seemed to follow paths I could not see as we traveled. Whether through dry land or wet, over hill or through dale, we always seemed to choose the better way of going, the route that provided the drier passage, the more moderate slope, the wider-spaced trees.

"The animals know how best to avoid impasses and dead ends," said Richard. "Look down. You will see their tracks. We walk where they do."

On the fifth day, we crested a low hill, still deep in the forest, and Richard ordered us all to stop. He then sent two men ahead and set out with several others in a different direction.

"We are in Mangoak country now," said Skiko. "The River of Death is that way, less than a day."

"Where they get their *wassador*," I said.

"Yes," said Skiko, nodding. "Their town of Chaunis Temoatan is there. Our two men will see how many Mangoaks are there now. Richard is setting out the others as guards, in case any of them are hunting in these woods."

Less than a day's walk from one of their principal towns? In Chowanoak, we foraged daily that close to town. I had been afraid for the entire trip, but was now doubly so.

The two scouts came back late in the afternoon. The town, they said, was surrounded by a strong palisade, but it was abandoned. All day they'd watched, and no one came or went. No smoke rose from within. No human sounds could they hear. Crows perched on the palisade and death birds circled overhead.

The men debated what that meant. Why would they abandon the town beside the river wherefrom they got their *wassador,* the source of their wealth? There was talk of the Mangoak collecting *wassador* from the river seasonally, when the flow was less rapid and the River of Death less likely to live up to its name—but that time of year was upon us. If they collected it when the flow was higher and more likely to dislodge the precious metal, that could explain their absence. Or perhaps they no longer gleaned it at all—maybe the *wassador* had all been collected.

Eventually, the men agreed that the answer, if there was one, could only lie inside the town itself. There was nothing for it but to go and look. Menatonan had sent us here to come back with answers, not questions.

At first light the next morning, we all went in: first a pair of scouts, who came back out to wave the all clear, and then the rest of us. The town inside the palisade was about the size of our own Citie of Raleigh on Roanoke. The huts were like all the other Indian dwellings I had already seen, framed with sapling trees and their rounded roofs and sides covered with woven mats. But all the huts here were closed—none of the side mats were rolled up. That I had never seen before. The Indians I knew only rolled them down in pouring rain. But there was something else.

The place smelled of death.

Richard, Skiko, and I stood in the center of the town while the other men cautiously approached the nearest closed hut. Before they got there, one of its hanging mats moved. The men froze and raised their weapons.

Out came a very old man, barely able to walk. He was followed by another old man, then an old woman. Soon, there were a dozen or more Mangoaks, all of them elderly and emaciated, more like cadavers than living people.

Our men lowered their weapons.

"What is this?" I asked of Richard.

He answered quietly, "When the land around a town can no longer supply enough food, the Mangoaks abandon the town and set out to find better land. The old and the feeble they leave behind."

"To die?"

Richard nodded. So did Skiko.

"But that's monstrous," I said.

"Our people once did the same," said Skiko. "It was the way of all the people in this world. But our crop fields are large and when the animals we hunt move to another forest, only our hunters need follow them. The hunters carry the meat back to all the people, including the old and feeble."

"And the Mangoaks do not?" I asked.

"The Mangoaks are savages," said Skiko. "That is why we fight them."

Then one of the old Mangoaks saw me. He cried out in a cracking, raspy voice as he pointed at me. The others, too, joined the cry. They started shambling toward us, like ghostly apparitions, holding out their enfeebled arms and mumbling words that I could not understand. I shrank back behind Richard and Skiko.

"Fear not," said Richard. "They cannot harm us. They are ancient and hold no weapons."

"Nor do they mean to," said Skiko. "They chant prayers."

When the dying ones reached us, they fell to their knees, reached out toward me and continued their mumbled chants.

"They think you are a spirit," said Skiko.

"What do I do?"

"I don't know," Skiko admitted.

"I do," said Richard. When I looked at him, he added, "Say the magic word. What we came here looking for."

"Try it," agreed Skiko. "Say it like a command. Raise your arm like my father does."

I raised my arm. The old people shrank in fear. I looked at Richard, then at Skiko. He nodded.

"*Wassador*," I said.

It was as if I had whipped them. Some cried out in despair. Others began to sob. A few just shook their heads. But one woman stood up. It was obviously a great effort for her, and when she finally got to her feet, she wavered on her spindly, ancient legs. But she did not fall. By her deeply wrinkled face, I guessed her to be the oldest one among them. She looked at me, then at Richard, then at Skiko. To Skiko, she said something in her language. He answered. She then turned and started slowly to walk away.

Skiko canted his head, telling us to follow her. We did. "What did she say?" I asked Skiko.

"She says you are not a spirit. She says she knows you are a person, but born without color, like a white deer or a white fox."

"Where is she taking us?"

"She did not say."

We followed her to one of the huts. Inside, she opened a large basket and retrieved from it an earthen jug the size of an English teapot. It had no lid, no opening at all. It did not appear heavy, but her wasted arms shook with the effort as she held it out toward me. I stepped forward to take it from her. She let it go.

With a muffled crack it broke open on the dirt floor.

"*Wassador*," she said.

Among the spilled contents were small pieces of wood and dried leaves, and a few small, shiny beads of irregular metal, each the size of a pea. Richard picked them up. They were less than a handful. Some seemed to be gold, others copper.

"*Wassador*," Skiko said. "That is how it comes from the river."

He turned to the old woman and spoke to her. She waved an unsteady hand at the nuggets held by Richard and answered. Skiko spoke sharply to her. She spoke again, drawing another sharp response from Skiko. She then sat down and began to chant.

Richard translated for me: "Skiko asked her where to find the rest of the *wassador*. She said there is no more, the river stopped giving, this is the last of it. Skiko demanded she tell the truth or he would have her killed. She said, 'I am already dead, we all are.' That's when she sat down." He looked to Skiko. "What do you think? Does she lie?"

Skiko squatted down in front of the old woman and looked steadily at her, the way his father had done to me when I said Manteo was our governor. "I think she tells the truth."

So did I. I held out my hand to Richard and he handed the *wassador* to me. I then squatted down before the old woman, took her hand, and gently placed the nuggets there.

"Rest in peace," I said.

The three of us left.

Outside, the old people continued to chant. On the palisade, crows had gathered, and overhead, dark vultures circled silently.

"Let us leave this place," said Skiko. "I have seen enough."

"And I," said Richard.

I had, as well. We returned to Chowanoak.

thirty-seven

When winter came, we moved away from Richard's house in town to live off the land. People did this every year, said Skiko, in order to find food, either moving inland to hunt game or downriver to the open water to seek shellfish, which is what Richard, Skiko, and I did. Anthony and William went inland with a different group.

We traveled with several dozen others. We went in canoes, traveling up and down the shoreline and stopping for a night or two here and there, depending on how many clams, oysters, and crabs we could gather in any one place before there were no more to be had. It was hard work, and it got harder as the water cooled, for one had to wade in the shallows for hours at a time, hunting for the shellfish we needed to survive. We all helped, men, women, and children old enough to stand in the water and carry a basket.

Though we did not always work in the water. One day, while the men worked in deeper water, we women went into the nearby forest to gather nuts and other late-season edibles. In order to do that, we had to disperse as we foraged. I engaged cheerfully in this task, wandering to and fro from tree to tree and keeping my eyes on the ground to scan for good things to add to my basket. I did not realize that I was alone until I turned around to return to the shoreline.

Anthony and William were there, grinning.

For a moment I was stunned speechless. How could this be? Then I recovered my senses, dropped my basket, and bolted. But Anthony was faster. He moved quickly sideways and blocked my path. I turned to run the other way and William cut me off. I was trapped.

They closed in on me, Anthony in front of me and William behind.

"Where did you come from?" I demanded. "What are you doing here?"

"We escaped," said Anthony. "And now you are coming with us."

"I am no—"

William clapped his hand over my mouth before I could make another sound. I wrenched and struggled, but to no avail—William was oxen strong. I could not even draw breath against his immovable arm around my midsection. Anthony stepped in front of me, grinning through his rotten teeth, and put one hand on my throat while a finger went again to his lips. William loosened his grip and removed his hand from my mouth. I gasped in a lungful of air. William grasped my arms, one of his iron hands clamping above each of my elbows. I may as well have been locked in stocks.

Anthony let go of my throat, then ran his finger down between my breasts to my deerskin apron. As if it were a cobweb, he snapped the leather thong that tied it around my waist.

"Richard will kill you for this," I hissed at him. "Both of you."

Anthony just smiled as he took off his own deerskin apron.

A sound came from the nearby trees, a keening female wail—then another, and another. The Indian women were there, all around us, a dozen of them crying out in their high-pitched, undulating voices as they moved slowly toward us. William let go of me and Anthony stepped back. The Indian women closed in, still wailing loudly, and Anthony lunged at them in retaliation. The women in that part of the circle fell back, never ceasing their cries. William lunged at another section and those women fell back as the other section came close again. All the time, their undulating wail reverberated through the forest, certain to be heard by the men.

William and Anthony looked at each other, nodded, and bolted together toward the circle of Indian women. The circle parted as the two men ran through it and kept going, fleeing deeper into the woods.

The Indian women gathered around me, either smiling or looking on with worry, until I smiled back. "Thank you," I said. "Thank you. Thank you. Thank you." One of them picked up my apron and tied a mend in its torn thong, then put it back on me. Another found my basket. We all then ran back to the shoreline.

Richard was beside himself. He wanted to set out after Anthony and William immediately. Skiko and I could never have deterred him, but there were twenty Indian men with us, all of them taller and some of them stronger than Richard, and many trained by Richard to fight in the English style. Skiko commanded them to stand in Richard's way, and even he could not fight his way through them. He eventually calmed down and came to his senses.

For the rest of the winter, we neither saw nor heard anything of the Englishmen. For my part, I certainly did not wander off alone again, but instead stayed close to the others as we all returned to the cold, dreary work of staying alive.

thirty-eight

In March, as we camped on the shore of the great sound on a very dark night, we were attacked by the Mangoaks. One minute, it was silent and pitch dark, and the next, there were whoops, wails, and great cries of agony as people were struck down, mingling with the sound of weapons clashing. Strong hands grasped me and pulled me away, then let go with a grunt of pain as other hands pulled me the other way. I kicked and pulled back until I worked myself free, was caught again, and then freed once more as my assailant was struck down, screaming in pain. I was completely disoriented and no doubt screaming, too.

And then I was with Richard and Skiko, the three of us running toward our canoes. Richard had his sharp wooden sword and hacked down any figures that came into our path. He was in an absolute frenzy and none who came before him remained standing. When we got to the canoes, he was covered in blood, none of it his. So violent were his strokes as he struck our enemies down, some of the blood had even splattered onto me.

We reached a canoe and all three of us paddled madly into the dark and away from the slaughter behind us. Eventually, we were clear of the scene, but we continued paddling all night, though I could not say where we were headed. There were no stars and I doubt even Simon Fernandez could have told us where we were.

At the first hint of dawn, I could see that we were on a large body of water, very similar to the one I had been on with Wanchese and his men when they had first ferried me toward Chowanoak. Richard and Skiko pulled us closer to the shore and soon found a small, vegetation-shrouded stream into which they paddled the canoe. While Richard grasped an overhanging tree branch to steady us, Skiko slipped out of the canoe and started back toward the mouth of the stream. It was still quite dark.

"Where is he going?" I asked.

"Back to the big water. When it gets light enough, he will study the shore to see where we are."

"Why didn't we just stay out there, then?"

"We want to see, not be seen. We have been paddling all night toward Wanchese's towns."

That sent a cold shudder through me. But then I realized something else: If we could get past the settlements of Wanchese, we would come to Roanoke Island. We would be safe.

As soon as there was faint daylight, Skiko was back, shivering from his immersion in the cold water. In the new world, spring has but barely begun in March.

"We cannot proceed in the canoe," he said through chattering teeth. "Wanchese's men are in their canoes. They do not fish. They watch, looking this way."

"He will have heard, then." Richard nodded. "He will know we must pass this way to reach the English."

"Yes," agreed Skiko. "But we do not have to pass by water. We can take the long way. We can go around Wanchese and his towns on foot."

"How far?" asked Richard.

Skiko considered. "His men will be watching in the forest, too," he finally said. "To be safe, we must go through the land where they will not be. Through the land of the red wolves."

"Wolves?" I said. "There are wolves in the new world?"

"I have seen their pelts," Richard said, "but I have never seen or heard one."

"Because we kill them whenever they come close to our towns," said Skiko. "Now they stay away. But in the land of the red wolves, the land is too low and wet to grow crops. There are no towns. In that land, the red wolves rule and the people stay away."

"I think that I would rather fight men than wolves," said Richard.

"We will be better to fight neither," said Skiko. "Both are far too many for just three of us."

"True," Richard agreed. "Then how do we avoid the red wolves?"

"With fire," said Skiko. "They are afraid of it. We will light a fire every night to keep them away. Wanchese's men will not be in that country, so the fire will not give us away."

What choice did we have? We set out as Skiko had recommended. I know not how heavy lay the sense of dread upon the spirits of Richard and Skiko, but upon mine, it was a leaden thing, cold and dark and growing more so with every step we took toward the land of the red wolves.

thirty-nine

For three days we walked through unbroken forest, heading, as far as I could tell from the rise and fall of the sun, first to the west and then to the south. As Skiko had promised, the ground became flatter and wetter. The deer trails we followed twisted and turned as dry ground grew scarce. Often we went for hours without finding any trail at all, sloshing through ankle- and waist-deep water.

In our flight from the Mangoak attack, Richard and Skiko had brought the weapons with which we had fought our way out, but naught else, and none of us carried food. So now we hunted. Skiko was an accomplished archer, as good with bow and arrow as was Richard with sword and axe, and I had already learned to skin and butcher. We wanted not for meat. Better yet, we could make a fire and cook it, for there were no adversaries here.

But there were wolves. On the third night, we heard them, their howling high-pitched and far away. Is there a more terrifying sound, especially when you lie not safely within your own closed house, but out on the ground in the darkened forest ruled by the wolves? When they grow silent for long periods and only your mind can hear them? Imagining their silent approach, eyes aglow and teeth bared, drooling and intent, driven by the same hunger that drove you in the daytime to hunt your own meat? Richard put more sticks on the fire and for the rest of the night we took turns keeping it blazing.

We heard them again the next night, and the night after that. Each time, they seemed closer.

"They hunt us now," said Skiko. "We leave a trail of our own kills, the parts of the deer we do not eat. They feast on our leavings."

"As long as they feast not on us," said Richard.

"Our fires will keep them away, will they not?" I asked.

"Yes," Skiko said, "but tomorrow we turn back toward the wide water. Across it will be the town of Croatoan, but on this side, it is still the land of Wanchese. To get safely to Manteo's people, we will have to get close enough to our enemies to steal one of their canoes. So after tonight we can light no more fires."

"But the wolves will still be with us," said Richard. "How many nights?"

Skiko considered. "One or two, I think. I am not sure. I only know this land by story, not by experience."

I was filled with dread the whole of the next day. I did not want the night to come; I spent my day looking up toward the sun, willing it to slow its passage. Of course, it did not.

Toward sunset, we came to a point of dry land surrounded on three sides by swamp. When we tried to cross the swamp, we discovered its water to be much deeper than it appeared. It required swimming to cross it, but only Skiko could swim.

"We'll have to go back to get around," he said. We turned back and retraced our route, walking into the deepening twilight.

That's when I saw the first wolf.

Richard and Skiko were intent on the path ahead, trying to hew as closely as they could to the preferred route of the deer, but my eyes were constantly shifting into the woods to our sides, ever alert for the wolves that had haunted me day and night since we came into this country. A flicker of movement caught my eye, then another.

A wolf, smaller than I had imagined, flitted through the trees, not a dozen yards away. I gasped.

"What?" breathed Richard.

"A wolf!"

"Where?"

I pointed. But it was gone. "Your imagination," he said.

"No! I saw it."

"Then we turn back," said Skiko. "They are upon us. Out on the point we will only have to defend in one direction."

"Sound plan," agreed a grim Richard.

We hurried back. Out on the point, the dry land was just a few yards wide. We sat close enough to reach out and touch one another, our backs to the last of the trees and facing the darkening forest, Richard on my right and Skiko on my left.

For an hour or more, nothing happened. The only sounds were our own breathing, the croaking of frogs out in the swamp, a call from a distant owl, and an occasional small splash behind us. I startled at every noise, real or imagined.

Then something moved in the forest. I felt it more than I heard it. So must have Skiko.

"They are here," he said quietly. "Growl at them."

"Growl?" I whispered.

"Like this." He emitted a low, menacing sound from deep in his throat.

From the forest came a return growl. I thought I might lose my continence.

Skiko growled again. So did the unseen wolf.

"I think it wants to fight," said Richard.

"No," said Skiko. "It wants to eat."

"Then it will have to fight first," said Richard. He jumped up and shouted, "Come and try me, wolf! Come and try me!" He struck his sword against the tree with a loud *clack!* Then again. *Clack! Clack! Clack!*

"Come and try me!"

There was silence.

"I don't think it wants to fight," said Richard.

"No," said Skiko. "But it still wants to eat."

From farther back in the trees, the wolf howled. The sound of it, so close, cleaved right through me. I shook, light-headed with fear. I don't doubt the other two felt the same.

Other wolves answered the first. They were farther away, but were soon in full voice, many of them.

"Now they come," said Skiko. "This one has called the others."

"What do we do?" I asked.

"Can you climb a tree?" asked Skiko.

"I used to be able to, when I was a child," I said. "Why?"

"Because the wolves cannot."

Richard nodded wryly. "Then up we go."

Skiko climbed one tree and Richard and I ascended together into another, driven from branch to branch by the nonstop howling and yipping of oncoming wolves. We got but ten feet off the ground before they arrived, a dozen or more of them, dark, fast-moving blurs, snarling and snapping beneath us as they tried to leap high enough to reach us with their teeth. They could not, and eventually they ceased their attempts.

But they did not leave. Though they were but indistinct shapes against the darkened ground beneath us, I could tell that some sat and looked up at us while others lay down. A few paced to and fro, lifting their snouts and sniffing the wind. The air soon filled with their own foul stink, a noxious mixture of carrion rot and swamp mud. How they could scent anything beyond their own overpowering odor was beyond me.

And thus we spent the rest of the horrific night, passing slowly through every ink-dark hour in a stalemate. The wolves were agitated, but comfortable, entirely at home. We were agitated and far from both comfort and home. I knew we could not remain long as we were. The wolves could certainly outlast us. I wondered if either Richard or Skiko had a plan.

The answer came with the first gray light of dawn. I heard the soft release of Skiko's bow and the muffled thud of one of his arrows striking a wolf. It yelped and spun in a circle, trying to bite at the arrow embedded in its body before collapsing and thrashing on the ground. The other wolves sprang to their feet and rushed about in confused chaos, barking.

Skiko shot another one. Now two were on the ground, in their death throes. That was enough for the others. They vanished like smoke into the woods. The two stricken wolves went still. In the ensuing silence, we waited until Skiko decided it was safe, then climbed down.

The two red wolves stank as much in death as they had in life, but they were clad in a wonderful fur, thick and soft and gray with a reddish blush from whence must have come their name.

"If we were in a safer land, we'd be rich," said Skiko. "These two pelts are worth their weight in *wassador.*"

Of course, we had to leave the dead wolves behind us, and so set out as we had the day before. We detected no wolves as we skirted the deep swamp and then turned back to the east, toward the wide water; toward Croatoan and Manteo; toward Roanoke and the English.

forty

Late the next day, we began to hear the cries of gulls and could smell the salt tang of the ocean. As it neared dark, we came to a small rise in the land just above a narrow beach and saw that we had finally made it to the wide water. Across it, in the fading light, I could see the low, dark smudge that I knew to be land.

"Croatoan," said Skiko. "We are almost there."

"But not quite," said Richard. "We still need to stay hidden."

We turned back into the forest and had only traveled a short distance when we came upon a most disturbing sight: a graveyard. An English graveyard with fifteen graves, each of them marked with a wooden Christian cross. And on each was carved a name.

We were stunned. Richard went to each grave, running his fingers over the carved names, then got down on one knee and bowed his head.

"I knew some of these names," he said. "They were on the fleet that brought us here, but they did not stay with us in the colony. They

194

went away with the ships that brought us. How came they here? How did they die?"

"The same as we," said a voice, weak and barely able to speak.

It was William's voice. Richard and Skiko got on either side of me and took up fighting stances. But it was near dark and we could not see anyone.

"Show yourself!" commanded Richard.

"Can't," croaked William.

"There!" said Skiko. He pointed to a pair of freshly dug graves on the other side of the makeshift graveyard. Cautiously, we approached, Richard and Skiko in front, me behind.

The two open graves were shallow. In one lay William; the other, Anthony. They were tied down to stakes, naked and unable to move, hollow-eyed and ashen-faced.

"Whose work is this?" demanded Richard.

"Wanchese's," said Skiko. "I have heard of this place, but thought it to be a fable."

"No fable," wheezed William. "Free us."

Richard and Skiko both looked to me. They did not have to speak their question. And sorely as it did tempt me to leave them, I did not—I *could* not. Could you? Though they were closer to animal than human, no living thing deserved to die like that, starved to death in their own graves. I nodded, and Richard and Skiko cut them free.

"Flee," said William. "Flee. They come at night."

"For what?" asked Richard.

"To see if we are dead yet. Go!"

With our new charges, we hurried back toward the wide water. It was dark by the time we got there. "We need a canoe," said Richard. William pointed and we followed his lead.

When we got close enough to the dark shapes of the beached canoes, Skiko stopped us. "I will steal one," he whispered. "In the dark I will seem one of their own."

Soon he was back with a canoe. But before we could get in it, a strong voice called out in English behind us, "Stop!"

Wanchese—and a dozen of his men, some carrying lit torches and others with drawn bows, their arrows pointed at us.

Skiko said something hurriedly in their own language, and Wanchese threw up his hand, stopping his men from harming us. He said something to Skiko.

"Yes, you know me," said Skiko. "I am Skiko, son of Menatonan!"

Wanchese spoke to his men. They lowered their bows. Wanchese pointed at William and Anthony, and they fell to their knees in supplication. He then pointed at the three of us.

"Stay on your feet," said Richard.

"Come here," said Wanchese, and we did as he commanded. "Tell me why I should not kill you," he continued, once we had assembled, and pointed first to Skiko.

"You already know why," said Skiko. "My father would send all of his men upon you and all of your men would die. All of your women and children would become his slaves. All of your towns would be his." He waved toward William and Anthony. "And you would die even more slowly than these two were meant to."

Wanchese pointed at me. "And you?"

I could only shake my head. Had I tried to speak, I doubt words would have come.

Wanchese looked at Richard. Richard turned to the other Indians and spoke directly to them in their language. He raised his sword and jumped at them. They jumped back in fear. Richard turned back to Wanchese.

Wanchese sneered. "They may believe that you are an unkillable Englishman, but I do not."

"Then order them to kill me," Richard replied. He turned back to Wanchese's men and stepped toward the Indians, who backed away.

"Appears you'll have to kill me yourself," said Richard.

Wanchese considered, then he said something to one of the torch-carrying Indians. The other man left at a run.

"At last," said Richard. "I've been waiting a long time for this." To me, he added, "Wanchese has sent for his sword."

196

In a moment, the Indian was back, but the sword he carried was not like Richard's. It was much longer and, when he handed it to Wanchese, the light from the flickering torches reflected from its shiny, gleaming blade. It was made of steel—an English sword.

"Where did you get that?" exclaimed Richard.

Wanchese smiled. "From a dead Englishman. One of the fifteen your two friends here were about to join when you interrupted their journey."

Richard turned to us. "Go!" he said. "In the canoe! Now!"

Anthony and William ran toward the canoe. Wanchese barked an order to his men, but Richard jumped toward them with his sword raised and they shrunk back.

"Go!" Richard commanded again. "Before they learn the truth!"

I started to protest. "But—"

"Go! Skiko, take her!"

Skiko took my arm and hustled me to the canoe. Anthony and William were already in it and starting to paddle away.

Wanchese shouted as he charged Richard with the English sword. Richard dodged the first swing.

"Go!"

Skiko helped me roughly into the canoe, then clambered aboard himself as William and Anthony paddled madly. I rolled to my knees and looked back as we pulled away into the darkness.

In the torchlight, Wanchese was wildly attacking Richard, chasing him with vicious swipes of the sword. Richard rushed in and struck Wanchese on the leg, knocking him down, but he leapt back to his feet and attacked again. Richard ducked the blade as it swept just over his head, then struck Wanchese again, now on the other leg, and drew blood. Wanchese again charged, though he was limping. He stumbled when he swung the steel sword and it struck Richard's wooden one, cutting it in twain. Richard threw it away and drew his knife instead, surging forward.

Wanchese turned the sword at the precise moment, so Richard took the blade deep into his middle. He stopped and dropped to his knees, blood gushing forth from the wound when Wanchese withdrew the sword. Richard remained on his knees.

"Don't look!" said Skiko. He pushed down my head. A great cheer went up from the Indians onshore. I pushed Skiko's hand away to look.

On the receding shoreline stood Wanchese, surrounded by his torch-holding men. In his hand was Richard's head, held high in the flickering light by his long blond hair.

My heart wanted to burst. My stomach wanted to disgorge. My voice wanted to scream. But, as in a dream, none of it happened. I could not make a sound. I could not breathe. I could not move. I could not even think.

Wanchese pointed at us. His men rushed to their canoes.

"Faster!" cried William.

"You two!" grunted Anthony. "Paddle!"

Skiko picked up a paddle and began. I was still too stricken to do anything. William thrust a paddle at me. "Paddle, you craven whore!" he shouted. "Or lose your head, too!"

A sudden hot rush came over me. I pulled my skinning knife and leapt at William with it. The canoe rocked wildly and my blade sliced down his chest, opening his skin but not sinking deep. He roared in pain and caught hold of me, and threw me overboard.

I thrashed in pure panic, inhaling water and coughing it out. Then, my feet struck the bottom. I steadied myself. The water was but shoulder-deep. But the footing was soft mud, and the night was dark and disorienting—I could barely keep myself upright even in the small waves.

A hand grasped my shoulder and I yelped in fear.

"It is I, Skiko!" He had dived in after me. "Stay quiet," he said. "The chasing canoes will pass this way!"

Soon they did, several of them, fast, dark silhouettes. They sped past us within a few yards, but only our heads were above water and it was very dark. They did not see us. And then they were gone.

"They will surely catch them," said Skiko. "We are lucky to be out of the canoe. Now we go to Croatoan."

"I cannot swim," I reminded him.

"Do not fear. We will get there."

Skiko took my hand and held it tightly while we slowly waded. When the bottom fell away and the water became too deep, he told me to get behind him and wrap my arms around his neck while he swam. When it became shallower, we waded again. Behind us lay the firelit nightmare of Wanchese and my poor, brave Richard. Somewhere out in the wide water were Anthony and William, one of them cut and bleeding, about to be recaptured and surely killed by Wanchese's men. But ahead lay safety: the comfort of Benginoor and the security of Manteo.

I know not how long it took—most of the night, at any rate. When we finally got close enough to shore, Skiko no longer had to steady me in the shallower water and I no longer had to fear the water suddenly rising over my head. I was able to calm myself enough to notice that as he moved through it, Skiko was leaving a glittering wake of phosphorescence.

I looked back to see that I, too, had left a shimmering trail. It was beautiful; I turned to show it to Richard. Then I cried for him. It makes me cry again now, as I write about the end of that good man, the father, as I was soon to learn, of my unborn child, the man who died to save us both. God rest him.

forty-one

After we reached his land and told him our story, Manteo brought me back here, to the island of Roanoke, to this hut, where I now write this journal. Again, he left me under the protection of two of his men, while he then went to the Citie of Raleigh to inform Ananias and the others that I had been rescued.

"You must wait here until I make certain you will be received safely there," he said.

"Why would I not?" I asked.

"Not everyone there believes you were taken, Emme," he explained. "Some say you went voluntarily with Wanchese, that you chose to live among us and not with your own people."

It was clear to me who believed such nonsense. "Elizabeth Glane and Elenora Dare."

"And Christopher Cooper," Manteo agreed, nodding. "He is gaining favor and is now a rival to Ananias for leadership. Your colony has become divided."

Several hours later, Manteo returned, Audry and Thomas with him. I was overjoyed to see them, especially Audry, but they both held back and Thomas averted his eyes.

Of course—I still wore only my deerskin apron. I had been among the Indians for so long that it seemed normal, though only to Manteo and me.

Audry handed Manteo the basket she carried and he passed it to me. Inside was a dress, freshly sewn. I held it up. It was lovely.

"The one I promised you," said Audry. "Do you still want it?"

"Oh, Audry, of course I do," I exclaimed. "Of course I do."

I went inside Manteo's hut and quickly put it on. It was a tight fit in my early—and still unknown—condition and it felt scratchy and uncomfortable after all those months of never wearing anything so confining, but I certainly did not say that to Audry when I came back outside.

"Thank you," I said. "It's perfect."

"You're welcome," she replied, then looked to her husband. "Thomas, you may look now."

He did, and they both relaxed visibly. Thomas smiled. "Welcome home, Emme."

I thanked Manteo again for all he'd done, and then Audry, Thomas, and I started down the two-mile path to town. I knew without looking back that Manteo had silently instructed his men to follow and guard us.

While we walked, I told Audry and Thomas my story. It took most of the way to town to complete it.

"And what of Skiko?" asked Audry when the tale was done. "What became of him after your rescue from Wanchese?"

"Manteo sent him back to his father. We parted fondly. I expect we will see much of him in the future, when he inherits the crown from his father."

"And the other two Englishmen?" asked Thomas. "What of them?"

"I know not," I answered. "But they must be dead. Manteo will tell us if he learns."

"If indeed we see him again," said Audry. "We may not. Cooper and his followers have a hardening attitude toward the Indians."

"But surely only toward Wanchese and his band," I said. "They're the ones we need to fear."

"All of them," Audry insisted. "They make no distinction."

"But that's—"

"Unfinished thinking," she interrupted. "I know. It's still rampant among us."

forty-two

As I walked through the palisade gate back into the Citie of Raleigh, people stopped what they were doing, looking up from tilling their garden plots or appearing in cottage or workshop doorways. Some smiled and nodded, others stared coldly. But no one spoke.

"Why are they silent?" I asked Audry as we walked toward her cottage.

"They're afraid," she said.

"Of me?"

She shook her head. "Of being wrong about you. Half believe Manteo's story that you were abducted. Half believe the other, that you went willingly. You can guess who's perpetrated the latter."

"Elizabeth and Elenora, I know. And Christopher Cooper, too, says Manteo."

"He's correct," she said, nodding. "But at least Master Cooper does not claim you're a witch. The man may be venal and cowardly, but he's not a fool."

I sighed. Audry and I had been with these people for too long not to know the truth. Many of them were all three of those.

For the next two weeks I kept company with Audry and Thomas. She and I went back to our previous work together, the cleaning and scaling of fish, and together we tended her assigned plot in the community garden. It was springtime now and there was much weeding and cultivating to do. In the evenings, we supped together. And through that entire period, I cannot say that I spoke more than a dozen words to anyone else, each word spent on simple responses to the rare one-word greetings from those not swayed by the sulking fulminations of my detractors.

Ananias I hardly saw. Elenora made sure of that, as did she with the baby Valentyne, now six months old. I was content not to see Ananias, as you will no doubt understand, but I longed to see Valentyne, and, of course, Elenora knew that. It must have given her great pleasure to keep him hidden from me. But at least I knew he was well, as Audry was allowed to see him and kept me informed. That was a small happiness.

I do not know how long I might have remained in that awkward situation, half a colonist among her people and half an outcast. Both Audry and I expected the collective distrust of me to abate over time, and had that prediction come true, then I am certain that I would have remained in town longer. As I hope you know by now, I am an optimist at heart, and never choose to dwell on the dark side of things. For those initial weeks back among my own kind, I was still that optimist.

But I failed to gauge how hot burned a hatred of me in the hearts of both Elenora and Elizabeth. They must have conspired nightly to drive me away. I shall not detail their whisperings here, however, for I am sure you will have no difficulty imagining them, and the time of the council is now upon me. All I have time to say is that, after a fortnight of trying, I gave up on the Citie of Raleigh. I thanked Audry and Thomas for their hospitality and support, and regretfully moved back here, to Manteo's hut. I do think it will be for the best, at least temporarily. Though I am not yet showing, soon enough it will be plain to all that I am with child. God alone knows how Elenora and Elizabeth will react to seeing that. Better to delay those insults as long as possible.

After today's council, I will return to this journal. Without the pressing demand of having to complete its narrative by an appointed time, I shall look forward to continuing it.

forty–three

The council has concluded and now I am back in Manteo's hut. It has been a long and most difficult two days, with an equally arduous night between. I barely have the strength to write, but I know that sleep will not come to me soon, if it comes at all. So I have once again picked up this quill and will now put it to paper.

Audry and Thomas came to fetch me for the council and, once again, we returned together to the town. By the time we got there, everyone had gathered in the community building. I assumed it to be June, for although the sun had only been up for an hour by the time we arrived, already the day was warm, only to get hotter. But it would have become just as insufferable inside the community building had it been deep winter, such was the vehemence of the debate that took place there over the last two days.

It began with Ananias stepping forward and raising his arms to quiet the hubbub, some of it directed at me as soon as I entered the building. Soon enough, he had the floor.

"My friends," he said, "we have visitors, and they have a report."

We all assumed they would be Indians from another band, so no one was surprised when Manteo appeared. But not one of us was prepared for the two men who followed him:

Anthony and William.

The collective gasp was audible, not least from me. The men were not dressed as Englishmen, nor were they as naked as when I had last seen them. Instead, they were resplendent in Indian finery, well covered in green-dyed deerskin and adorned with beadwork and necklaces and armbands of shining golden metal.

"Do not be misled by their attire," Ananias managed to say over the chatter the new arrivals had caused. "These two are William Backhouse and Anthony Rottenbury, two of Grenville's men who were left here to secure this citie when Sir Richard sailed back to England. You will recall that our former governor, John White, came ashore here first to make contact with them, but failed to do so. We now know why, as these two will explain."

He stepped aside and William came forward. I tried to catch his eye, but was unable to do so before he spoke.

"My friends, we come to you with wonderful news," he began. "But first, let me offer an apology and explanation for what may have at first seemed to you all to be a dereliction of our duty to remain here and protect this town."

The words flowed from William's evil mouth as smoothly as from any man I had ever heard speak. He walked to the center of the room and looked around.

"And a fine town it is," he continued. "You are all to be commended for the hard work it must have taken to restore and improve it."

He bowed and was rewarded with smiles and grateful nods in return—from some, though not all. And certainly not from me.

"But," he resumed, "I must in all honesty report to you that your work has been unnecessary. There are great riches waiting for us all farther inland, in a beautiful land up the great river from which Anthony and I have just returned."

The crowd erupted with astonished responses. I tugged on Audry's arm urgently and shook my head at her. She nodded and knit her brow, skeptical as ever, I was relieved to see.

William raised his hands for quiet, then went on. "The Indians there are most friendly and hospitable. Because the land is so fertile, the water so sweet, and the streams so lined with this golden metal they call '*wassador*' . . ."

He paused to show off his shining armbands. "They have little need to toil. Instead they dance and play games, sing and make artwork. We live like kings among them. And so can you all. Kings and queens, I say. All you need do is come with us. Anthony and I will lead you all away from this dreary fortified village and into the open place you will immediately recognize as the Promised Land."

I could no longer stand to hear it. I pushed forward to confront him. It was his turn to be astonished. Quickly, he turned to Anthony, who was equally taken aback. Both went mute, their eyes wide in surprise. I didn't wait for either of them to speak.

"William Backhouse, you are a liar," I said. "And if you support him, Anthony Rottenbury, then you are, too." I turned to the colonists. "These two were slaves in the village where I was held, condemned to hard labor and living like dogs. As was I. When last I saw them, naught but a month ago, they were fleeing for their lives from Wanchese's men. How they came to this, I cannot say, but it can only be a ruse. There is no place such as the one William has just described. The Indians live in villages like the ones near here. They toil as hard as we do, just to keep themselves in food and shelter. This is a monstrous lie."

Everyone broke into shouts and murmurs and confusion. I looked at Anthony and William, now huddled together in hurried conference. Ananias stepped forward and quieted the room.

"Hear me," he insisted. "Mrs. Merrimoth, please stand where you are. And you two, Backhouse and Rottenbury, stand forward and face your accuser. What say you, is it true what she says?"

Anthony and William hurriedly finished their huddle and came forward. This time it was Anthony who spoke. "Milord, we do not know this woman. We've never seen her before."

I was shocked. "You are lying—"

"But we have heard of her, milord," Anthony interjected. "She were living in a different Indian town as we. And she was a harlot to the Indians, sir. By her own choice."

"What?" I shouted.

"I knew it!" called out Elizabeth Glane.

"As did I!" said Elenora Dare.

"Silence!" Ananias called out. Then he said to Anthony, "Go on, man."

"No!" I shouted. "It's a lie! He cannot—"

"Silence, Mrs. Merrimoth!" commanded Ananias. "You shall have your turn!"

"Thank you, milord," said Anthony, all the time looking directly at me. "As I told, we knew of her. She was with a different band than us, one nearer to here, in a town called Chowanoak. Those people are not friendly like the ones me and William were among. The town we can show you, the land of the Mangoaks, milord, is indeed the Promised Land, like William has told."

Ananias turned to me. "Mrs. Merrimoth, you may now respond."

I had begun to shake with fury as Anthony spoke. My face was flushed, my breath coming in forced heaves. It was a rising anger, the like of which I had never felt before. I clenched my teeth and forced myself to speak clearly.

"This . . . this is the most monstrous, the most *evil* set of lies I have ever heard. Anywhere. Not one word of any of it is true. Not one word!" I turned to Ananias. "You cannot, you must not believe them! Where these lies come from, or why they are being told, I cannot guess. But they are—"

209

"Be silent, harlot!" shouted Elizabeth. "Go back to your Indians!"

Ananias raised his hand, but before he could admonish her, I did it myself.

"Elizabeth Glane, you be silent!" I shouted. "I have never been a harlot! I did not choose to live with the Indians! And unlike you, I have never told a vicious lie before this council. Were I a man, I would fight you with my own bare hands. If you utter one more ignorant lie, I may still. Do you hear me? Do you?"

Ananias stepped between us. "Enough! Mrs. Merrimoth, please control yourself. Mrs. Glane, please remain silent until called upon. Now—"

"Now I will speak," interrupted Manteo. The room fell silent as he stepped forward. "Some of my men of Croatoan found these two Englishmen in their canoe," he explained. "They were not dressed as they are now. They told my men they were coming here, to your citie, and my men first brought them to me. I then brought them here. Now I see them dressed like this and I hear their story for the first time. The people they tell of, the Mangoaks, are real. They do live far up a great river. But it is the River of Death. The Mangoaks are very dangerous and warlike. We have all fought with them many times, even Wanchese and his men. Their land is not like the Promised Land of your Bible."

Ananias pointed at Anthony. "What say you to that, man?"

Anthony turned to William, who bowed slightly to Manteo and then said, "In the land of the Mangoaks, we have heard of your return from England. We have heard that you are now king in this part of the world, appointed by Her Majesty by way of Sir Walter Raleigh. We, too, accept your dominion here. But in the land of the Mangoaks, we have no king. Each of us is lord of his own dominion, the king of his own household. So it is with great respect and deference that I say to you, sir, that you are not the king of me and Anthony, nor are you the king of anyone who chooses to live in the land of the Mangoaks. For in that place there is no king, nor is there a queen. We are all free men and women."

William turned to the gathering. "Come with Anthony and me, I say. Come with us to a paradise where you will live free and rich, like Anthony and me. Leave this dreary place to Manteo and his people. Let him and his people believe what they want about the Mangoaks. He is wrong. The Mangoaks fight with no one. It is the Indians near here who fight with each other all the time, because it is the only way they know. Their life, like your life here, is too hard. Come with us to a place where no one will ever be your king, Indian or English."

People nodded in agreement and broke into small groups to talk, ignoring Ananias's calls for order.

It was like a nightmare—Manteo had told the truth and Anthony and William had told a lie, but many seemed to believe the lie. And there was nothing I could do to sway them. I looked around in stunned silence until Audry tapped me on the shoulder.

"It is a lie, is it not?"

I nodded. "Every word. But why are they telling it?"

"Who can know? Maybe they're simply addled. But whatever the reason, you must do something. These fools believe them. They've bought them with their own prejudice."

I gathered myself and walked over to Manteo. "Please make them quiet," I said. "We must convince them of the truth."

"Yes, we must." He called out, "Silence! Now!"

Despite the strong words against Manteo, his voice, loud and commanding, had its effect.

"Now," he said. "Hear the truth. These men lie. They will lead you to certain death. If Wanchese's men do not kill you like they killed Grenville's fifteen, then the Mangoaks surely will. Your only safety is here, under my protection. Perhaps later, when more English come to join you and you are strong enough, then you can move this citie to some other place. But not before. You are few and the Mangoaks are many. You will have no chance."

"Of course this Indian wants you to stay here under his command," William spoke up. "And he lies about Grenville's fifteen. They are all alive and living among the Mangoaks with Anthony and me. Who would know more about that, this Indian or the two of us? They were our mates and they still are. Come with us and see for yourselves."

"'Tis not true," I said. "The fifteen are all dead. I have seen their graves, as these two men have. They died horribly, starved to death by Wanchese. Anthony and William were already in their graves when Richard freed them and saved their miserable lives!"

"Who is Richard?" asked Ananias. Most of the others were just as puzzled. Of course, I realized, I had only told Audry and Thomas of him—no one else.

"Ask them," I said. "Ask these two about Richard Poore, the Englishman who was their friend. The Englishman who was by far their better. The Englishman who saved them—and me—from Wanchese and his people, and died doing it. The Englishman whose child I now carry. Ask them about him!"

I know not what caused the greater astonishment, my revelation that there had been another Englishman among the Indians or that I was now carrying his child, something I had only just learned myself. In any case, it caused a great din of conversation and questions that required the repeated demands of both Manteo and Ananias to quell. But eventually civility returned.

"I shall do precisely that," Ananias said. "Backhouse and Rottenbury, who was this man Poore?"

Once again Anthony and William engaged in a hurried, whispered colloquy. It was too much for me to bear. "Look at them," I said. "Can you all not see how they conspire to concoct a new story every time they are challenged?"

"Not so," said Anthony. "The new stories keep coming to us from this woman and your Indian governor. We are just asking each other if one of us has heard them before. So far, we have not."

"Are you saying you have never heard of Richard?" I demanded.

"No, he was one of us, milord," said William. "Originally. But he never made it to the land of the Mangoaks. He was captured by the same Indians she was a harlot to, so maybe she was a harlot to him, too. Me and Anthony don't know anything about that, how he might have died. He was our friend long ago, but we ain't seen him since we found the land of the Mangoaks. So God rest him, then, if he has passed."

Behind him, Anthony nodded in agreement. Then they both looked at me with pity. The anger flowed over me again, even stronger. But this time, it made me quiet. I walked over to them, shaking with rage but still in control.

"You don't know anything about Richard and me?" I asked. "Is that what you claim?"

"Yes, mum," said William. "Because it is the truth. We never seen you before today."

"Then tell me—no, tell all these good people—why it is that I know of the mark that you carry. The long cut from a knife that runs from your throat to your belly. The one I gave you myself!"

William turned in panic to Anthony. Anthony shook his head at me. "There is no scar, madam, on my friend. We know not whereof you speak."

"Then open your shirt," I demanded. "Let everyone see and decide for themselves who is lying here."

"Madam, he cannot. It would be indecent in mixed company."

"Not to her!" called out Elenora.

There was quiet laughter from a few of the onlookers, though most remained silent, knowing, I hoped and prayed, how serious this was. I turned pleading eyes to Ananias.

He turned to the two. "We must know the truth here. We have all lived in very close quarters together for quite some time. I feel confident that none of the ladies present will be offended if you do open your shirt to either prove or disprove Mrs. Merrimoth's claim."

William and Anthony looked at each other, then William reluctantly opened his shirt. The cut I'd left in his flesh ran livid and bright down his chest.

A collective gasp ran through the room, followed almost instantly by a scream of fear from William.

"Witchcraft!" he said. "She's marked me!"

Elizabeth got to her feet. "I knew it!"

Pandemonium broke out, unable to be controlled, cries to seize me, to show mercy, to be silent.

Manteo broke through. He waded into the middle of the tumult, raised his arms high above the crowd, and boomed, "Be silent." The room grew quiet and he continued, "Hear me! There will be no talk of witches here. As I before decreed, no one will stand accused of witchcraft in this land. Any colonist who accuses another of witchery shall be punished." He turned to William. "You have been warned."

"Yes, milord," said William, nodding vehemently. Anthony nodded, too.

"You say this mark is new?" Manteo pressed. "That you have never seen it before? Is that what you claim?"

"Yes, milord," said William. "It just appeared, sir. I don't know how she—"

"Silence," Manteo interrupted. He turned to me. "Mrs. Merrimoth, please speak."

Still reeling from the men's denials, my breathing labored, I felt slightly nauseous, almost too ill to stand, as any woman who has been early with child will certainly understand.

"I did make that mark on him," I managed to say, "but not by magic. I cut him with my knife the night my Richard died saving his worthless life. I was trying to kill him, but I failed. Would that I had not."

"But it's not true—" protested Anthony.

"She is a savage!" cried Elizabeth.

"You have had your turn to speak," Manteo said, demanding silence. He then looked to Ananias. "I turn this meeting back to you. You know your people better than I. I shall let you guide them to their decision."

"Thank you," said Ananias. "But before we continue, I suggest we take a recess to gather our thoughts. Some of you will certainly wish to discuss in private. We shall reconvene in two hours' time."

Manteo left for his hut and the rest of us dispersed. Thomas, Audry, and I repaired to their cottage.

"They are in the majority," said Audry. "The fools will carry the day."

"But what will that mean?" I asked. "Will we be forced to go with them, or can we remain here?"

"No one will dare split the colony," said Thomas. "Even the fools will understand the danger in that, not to mention the inefficiency. We only have one blacksmith, two coopers, a handful of sailors, and not many competent with arms."

"Why will they need arms?" Audry sneered. "Everything up the great river is sweetness and light."

"Should the colony vote to follow these two," Thomas continued, "Ananias will accede to that vote. But he will also require that we all go."

I sighed. "Let's hope he can dissuade the others from their self-destructive folly."

We three looked at one another for a moment, then shook our heads. "He will not dissuade them," said Audry. "They believe what they wish for, not what they see. Rottenbury and Backhouse are lying, but the fable they tell is one fools want to believe."

"But why are they lying?" said Thomas. "What could be their purpose?"

"We must talk to Manteo," I said. "His men found them. He may know more."

"Agreed," said Audry.

"Then let's go to Manteo immediately," said Thomas. "We have scant time."

Manteo's sentries met us halfway along the path and escorted us to the hut. One of the guards ran ahead to let him know we were en route, so he was waiting for us when we arrived.

"I know why you have come," said Manteo. "But I have no answers for you. Wanchese is now my enemy, and everything he does in his towns is kept secret from me. But we must assume that Wanchese's men did recapture those two on the night you and Skiko escaped. He must have allowed them to come here."

I was perplexed. "I don't understand. Why would Wanchese do that?"

"I believe he is now using them as bait," Manteo said gravely.

"To lure us English away from your protection," gasped Audrey.

"But why would William and Anthony allow themselves to be used like that?" Thomas asked.

"Wanchese has been gathering support among the other local people to start a war against my people and yours," Manteo explained. "He has been gaining strength. If he convinced the two Englishmen that they and all the rest of you English were soon to be killed, and he then offered them salvation, they might agree to lure the English out of my protection to save themselves."

Audry turned to me. "You know the two of them. Might they accept such an arrangement?"

"They are the vilest, most evil men I have ever known," I said. "And they are cowards."

"Then it is probably true," Thomas agreed.

"What can we do?" I asked.

"Everything in your power," Manteo intoned. "The colony must not be allowed to follow these two. I doubt they will listen to me. It must be your words that sway them."

When our conversation had ended, we returned to the citie, Manteo with us. As everyone gathered in the community building, Audry and I spotted Christopher Cooper walking in with William and Anthony, the three of them deep in conversation.

"I don't like the look of that," she said.

"No," I agreed. "They're simply dangerous, but he's smart. Nothing good can come of that."

When the council resumed, Ananias first called upon Manteo. "We know you to be a man of judgment," he said. "You certainly know the other Indian peoples better than do we. You have heard the competing claims. I would ask you first: Whose tale should we believe, Rottenbury and Backhouse or Mrs. Merrimoth?"

"I would not believe these two," Manteo said, pointing at William and Anthony. "Everything they say about the Mangoaks is untrue."

Then Christopher Cooper asked to speak, and Ananias gave him the floor.

"My friends, hear me," he said, unctuous as always. "I have listened to the arguments made this morning, and have spent these last two hours questioning Masters Backhouse and Rottenbury. As you all know, I am a solicitor and a warden, and I have interrogated many a witness in my time. You should heed my counsel now.

"Our governor, the Indian Manteo, who was chosen by none of us, wants us to believe him. He wants us to remain here as his serfs and chattel. I think, therefore, that he is not to be believed. In opposition, we have two Englishmen, two of our very own, who have come to us to explain what they have seen with their own eyes. They have no other motivation but loyalty and generosity toward their own kind. And these two tell the truth. I stake my reputation on it."

Audry drew a sharp breath. "They've taken him into the plot. He's saving his own skin."

Cooper relinquished the floor to resounding applause and cries of, "Hear, hear!"

He had turned the tide. The tally was certain now. All that remained were another two hours of impassioned debate that changed no mind. Manteo was particularly eloquent and persuasive, I thought, but Audry and Thomas were right—most in the colony had closed their ears, and their minds, to any Indian's words.

The final vote had two thirds in favor of leaving. As soon as it was done, about midday, people began to leave the community building to prepare for the next steps. But Elenora and Elizabeth stopped them.

"Wait!" Elenora called out. "We have something to decide."

"The harlot," agreed Elizabeth. "Must we suffer her to remain among us, or should we leave her here with her Indians?"

I stepped forward immediately. "Suffer not, Elizabeth Glane, nor any of the rest of you. I shall not be leaving this island with you. I have seen with my own eyes the fate that awaits you all at the hands of Wanchese and his men. I intend to stay alive. I intend to bring my baby into this world safely."

"Hah! She is one of them now." Elenora snorted. "Leave her and her heathen spawn here. We shall be well gone."

To my—and everyone else's—astonishment, Audry then proclaimed, "And I shall be staying here with her."

"You shall not!" shouted Thomas.

"Thomas, we have discussed this and my mind is firm," she replied. "I know you agree with me that following those two charlatans is folly, that it will be the death of them all."

"I do," he answered. "I agree with you totally. But we are part of this colony and sworn to live by its choices."

"Not I," said Audry.

"Yes," said Thomas. "You." He took her firmly by the elbow to lead her away.

"Wait!" I called out, and they stopped. "Please, Thomas," I pleaded. "Please, change your mind. Remain here with Audry!"

I turned to Ananias. "Let them stay. We can wait here for when the next English ship arrives. We can then tell them where you went. They might even arrive in time to save you!"

To his great credit, a small thing to remember him by, Ananias did not reply at once. He looked long and hard at me, then at Thomas and Audry, then back to me.

"No," he said sadly. "You, Mrs. Merrimoth, will be allowed to remain here. That I have already decided, based on your unusual circumstances. But you will remain here alone—"

"Good!" interrupted Elizabeth. "Let the—"

Ananias spun on her. "Silence, Mrs. Glane!" he hissed, as angry as any of us had ever seen him. "One more evil word from you and you shall stay with her! We would all be far better off without the constant bile from your dishonest mouth, so do not doubt that I shall issue that order instantly upon the next sound it utters. Do I make myself clear? Nod your understanding, and then leave us! Not a sound!"

She nodded meekly and shrank away.

Ananias turned back to me. I could see small tears in his eyes. "Manteo's mother will care for you, and for your child should it be born alive," he said, his voice much softer now. "Go with Manteo to her at Croatoan. We all wish you good fortune, and do hope to see you again. Meanwhile, should replenishments arrive from England, you can, as you say, direct them to us up the great river in the land of the Mangoaks."

They both turned to go. Most of the others followed, though not Audry. She kept her eyes on me.

"There is one more thing," she said. "If Emme goes with Manteo to Croatoan and we have left, how will our replenishers know what to do when they arrive? No one will be here."

"Readily solved," said Christopher Cooper. "Anthony, William, and I have already considered it. We shall leave a signpost for them."

"Saying what?" replied Audry. "That we have all gone to the land of milk and honey? That should help immensely."

"Hold your tongue," Thomas admonished.

But Cooper waved him away and replied, "It shall read, 'Find us up the great river in the land of the Mangoaks.' That will lead them to us."

"To our graves, you mean," Audry muttered, then said louder, "Carve 'Croatoan' on it. Someone among the replenishers will already know where that is." She turned back to me. "And there they will find my friend Emme Merrimoth—my greatest friend and her new baby, the one none of us will ever take from her."

We looked at each other through brimming eyes. I sorely wanted to embrace her, as I expect she did me, but we did not. The distance between us was now too great, the time too short. Again, Thomas took her by the elbow, but this time she gathered herself, gave me one last smile, and left.

Soon, only Ananias and Elenora remained. Ananias smiled at me. "Wish us Godspeed?"

I forced a smiled in return. "Of course," I said. "Godspeed to you, Ananias."

That was too much for Elenora. Ananias had not told her to be silent. "I have a question for the harlot," she said.

"Only if you address her by her proper name," said Ananias. He kept his eyes on mine. "Otherwise, you will remain silent."

"Emme Merrimoth," she forced herself to say, "tell me this. If ships do come, but they are the Spanish seeking to destroy us, what will you tell them? Will you sell us out to our enemies?"

I didn't look at her, instead keeping my eyes on Ananias's. "How could I do that, Mrs. Dare, when it has already happened? I would only be able to tell them what I will have to tell the English—that I am the only one left."

forty-four

How should I have dealt with a dilemma as great as this?

The colony had just been shown two paths but had chosen the wrong one, the one that would surely lead them to their doom. I knew where that path led but my fellow colonists did not. They had chosen to follow a pair of false guides, evil men intent on leading them away from their own safety solely in order to enhance their own.

What, then, should I have done? What would you have done? Let all your friends unknowingly choose the path to their own destruction? Or would you take stronger action to save them?

I took stronger action. How could I not?

The night after the end of the council, while the other colonists began packing their belongings and preparing to depart for the unknown, I returned to Manteo's hut. I was effectively banished from the colony, so it was the only place for me to go. But I would have gone there anyway—it suited my plan.

Manteo was there, alone. In his hut, I took off my English dress and put on my deerskin apron. Manteo watched with curiosity.

"You do not need to do that," he said. "You may remain as an Englishwoman while you await the next colony."

"Thank you," I said. "I will do that. But not tonight. Tonight, I need to be dressed as an Indian. May I have a skinning knife?"

"What are your intentions?" he asked.

"You said the colony must not be allowed to follow William and Anthony."

"I did."

"I am going to see that they cannot."

"How will you do that?"

"I cannot say."

He nodded and handed me a knife. He then went to a large basket, reached in, and pulled out my black feather cloak, the one that Richard had given me. "And you will need this."

"Where did you get that?" I gasped.

"Skiko sent it to me, after he returned to Chowanoak. His message was to give it to you in memory of Richard Poore."

"Skiko returned home safely?" I said.

"He did. But he can no longer pass through Wanchese's waters without a fight, or he would have delivered it himself." Manteo held out the cloak and I stepped into it. "You know how to use it, then," he noted.

I nodded. "My husband taught me well. I have used it many times. I was never seen."

"Then use it well, Emme Merrimoth," he said. "Whatever you do, no harm will come to you afterward. You have my promise."

"Thank you."

I then left.

You understand my intentions as well as Manteo did, don't you? I say that here because I do not wish to commit them to paper. I am not an evil person. I have never plotted evil toward anyone, save for that one night. And even then, as I slipped, dark-clad and silent through the moonless night, back toward the cottage wherein I knew slept Anthony and William, my thoughts were not upon what I meant to do once I got there, but instead dwelt upon the joy I would feel when the colony did not embark on its doomed journey. For without those two false guides to lead them, they would have no choice but to remain here.

As I neared the village's palisade gate, I slowed. Sentries would be posted, as they always were. But the night was dark; I knew I was all but invisible whenever I held still. Richard had taught me how to remain as low as possible whenever I did move, one step at a time followed by a period of absolute stillness. It takes a very long time to cover very little ground that way, but the hour that it took for me to traverse from the edge of the forest, through the clearing, to the gate was to my advantage. By the time I got inside the palisade, the village had stilled. Everyone was finally asleep.

William and Anthony were staying in the cottage of Christopher Cooper. When I got to the adjacent cottage, I stopped to listen. Inside Cooper's, I could hear the men snoring. But in the quiet, I could also hear my own heart, beating loudly. My head swam with nerves and fear; my legs quivered. My hand shook as I reached inside the cloak to retrieve the knife from inside my apron.

I steeled myself with resolve and started forward.

"Hssst!" From behind me.

I nearly cried out, almost dropped the knife. I spun to face my adversary.

It was Audry. She wore a black dress and veil. Though not as invisible as I, she was nearly so.

"Audry?" I whispered.

"Emme?" she whispered back. "'Tis you?"

"'Tis I." I pulled back my feathered hood.

She came close. "I knew someone might try something like this," she whispered. "But I assumed it would be a man."

"What are you doing here?" I whispered.

"Not the same as you, for certain. I am no murderess."

"Then go home," I said. "Pretend you never saw me."

"I cannot. You mustn't do this. It is a crime and a sin and you will hang for it."

"Manteo says not."

"Manteo is a heathen. He is wrong."

"He is our governor."

"It matters not who he is, Emme. He is wrong."

"Go home, Audry," I said again. "Do not try to stop me." I started toward the cottage.

"I shall cry out if you proceed."

I had to stop. "Please, let me do this. I don't want the others to die. I don't want you to die."

I started again, but she stepped in front of me. "And I do not want you to die, Emme, nor to suffer eternal damnation for murder. I will not let you do it."

Now I was so frustrated I was near tears. "On pain of your own death?" I demanded. "Of Thomas's? Of Ananias's and everyone else's? Who are you to play God, Audry? Who are you to decide for so many others whether they live or die?"

"I am the same as you—no one to decide God's will. But neither are you."

Now I was crying, and I could hear in her voice that she was, too.

"I am going to cut their throats, Audry. I don't care if I go to Hell. I don't care if I hang."

"And your unborn baby?" she asked.

All I could do was look at her. How could I have gotten this far without considering that? I put the knife away and drew a long breath. In all the time I had known Audry, in all the hours we had talked together, worked together, shared together—both good and bad—I had never once bested her in an argument, nor come to a better answer to a problem than she. In every way I knew, she was a better person than I. And she was again this night, as she stood between me and an act I cannot even bring myself to write on this, a sheet of paper onto which my tears now fall as I record these, the last words she ever spoke to me, and I to her.

"Come," she said. "I shall walk you to the gate." After a few steps, Audry said, "No more need for stealth, so you can remove that preposterous bird costume."

I took it off.

"Oh," she said as she looked away in embarrassment. "On second thought, put it back on."

I smiled through my tears and put it back on.

"I shall miss you," she said. "Very much."

"And I you," I responded. "Even more."

We got to the gate.

"I love you, Emme Merrimoth," she said. "God save you."

"And God save you, too, Audry Tappan. I love you, too."

forty-five

Would I have killed them? Would that I had. Surely they deserved it. But could I have? I do not really know, though I know I would have surely tried.

In my mind, first as I planned the deed and again as I walked back to Manteo's hut in the night with the deed undone, I saw myself doing it. As soon as I was in the room where they slept, I would shed the feather cloak. With just the knife in my hands, I would creep silently forward, pausing at the first sign of wakefulness from either of them, rigid and unmoving, as Richard had taught me. Once at William's bedside—I had decided to kill him first, because he was so strong that I feared him awake more than Anthony—I would quickly slit his throat, then rush over to Anthony and do the same, before any thrashing or sound from William might awaken him. Christopher Cooper I would leave alone. Without the other two, he was no danger to the colony, and unlike the other two, he had attempted no bodily harm against me.

But Audry, in full knowledge of what she was doing, had stopped me, almost certainly giving up her own life in order to save mine. Can a greater sacrifice be made by a living person? Is that what a saint does? I do not know. I have never been a churchgoer, as you undoubtedly know by now, so my understanding of such things is limited.

No matter now. It is done, or, rather, undone, and the chance will not come again.

forty-six

They are all gone. I am here alone. Or, I should say, alone as an Englishwoman. Manteo and his men wait outside this hut while I finish this writing.

They left this morning. All of the women and children, and some of the men, went in the pinnace *Plumrose,* the rest of the men in canoes, paddling beside. I suppose that once upon a time it would have been a lovely sight, the white sails and flying pennants of the pinnace, the dipping and flashing of the paddles.

But it was not. I stood forlornly on the shore and watched through crying eyes as the tiny flotilla of my fellow countrymen grew smaller and smaller across the wide water until, finally, it vanished altogether—first the canoes and then the mast of the *Plumrose,* the last flash of its topmost sail disappearing without a sound below the dark smudge of the far horizon.

How could I not recall Simon Fernandez's warning to me, when we stood on his deck and he steered my eyes in this same direction and predicted exactly this, the disappearance of us all into an unknown, unlit land?

Though not all. I am here, am I not? I write in this journal. And you do read it, do you not? So for now, I will close it. Manteo and his men wait. My unborn child waits. It is time for me to take leave of this place, this Roanoke. I do not know when, or if, I shall see it again.

forty-seven

I write again.

Two years have passed since last I took this quill in hand, since last I opened the sheaves of this journal. But something important is about to happen and I must record it.

This morning, sails appeared on the ocean horizon, heading northward and passing too far away to tell if they were English or Spanish ships. The whole village rushed down to the shore and watched for an hour or more, until the sails had passed from our sight. We could not tell how many they were, as even the closest few were so far offshore that only their masts and sails were visible to us above the horizon.

"What, Mommy?" asked Chance. "What?"

An error. My journal writing skills have withered, clearly. I haven't yet written about my son, have I?

His name is Chance. He is nearly two years old, blond and blue-eyed, healthy, and growing fast toward the likeness of his father, Richard, God rest him. Though the Indians do not use last names and he is only Chance to them, he is Chance Poore to me. And to himself—already he is learning to say it.

It is August, I am quite certain. Certainly it is high summer, and hot. All of Benginoor's people still live together here on Croatoan, since there is abundant food to be so easily gathered and harvested at this time of year. Chance is learning to gather mussels and, like the Indian children, he loves to chase crabs and try to catch them, too. He is a happy child. He laughs all the time. And it makes me laugh with him when he does.

But I cannot say that I am happy. Contented, I suppose. Though never far from my mind are thoughts of Audry and the others.

I hasten to write that I do not know for certain what became of them. We hear conflicting stories. In the beginning, I relied upon Manteo retelling them to me, but it took me not more than a few months to gain enough of the language to be able to listen for myself whenever some of the men returned from across the wide water with their reports and rumors.

This much is certain: They did not find the paradise for which they searched. Everyone here knows that was a lie. And everyone here now knows to be true what Manteo had originally surmised, that Wanchese was behind the plot. Wanchese himself continues to boast of it. That I have heard for myself.

Sometime last year, once Chance was old enough to travel with me, Manteo and several *weroances* took us to see Wanchese. We traveled by canoe and met on a neutral island whose name I never knew. Manteo wanted Wanchese to know that not all the English had fallen for his ruse, that I was still here and would relate the tale of his perfidy to the next group of colonists, who were sure to come soon.

Wanchese was unchanged when we met. His eyes still burned with hatred for me as an Englishwoman, but Manteo and his men had chosen the place of our meeting well. Wanchese had no choice but to see for himself that not only was I alive, my baby was, too. The next colony would certainly believe everything I had to tell them.

"And what will you tell them, Englishwoman?" he asked.

"That Manteo is their friend and that you are their enemy," I replied. "I will tell them that you are guilty of the killing of all their predecessors. I will warn them against the lies you tell. And I will tell them to greet those lies with force of arms."

"But I am not guilty of what you say," he said. "Yes, it was I who lured them away, but my people killed none of them. I did not want the English dead, I just wanted them gone. I did not want them making their colony in my country. I granted them free passage on their way inland."

"Then tell me what became of them," I demanded.

"I do not know," he said. "No one knows. They have gone somewhere unknown to us, unknown to any of the people around here. Very far away."

"Another lie," I said to him, and stood. The Indians did, too. I continued, looking right at Wanchese, "The father of my son died saving me, and his unborn son, from you. I cannot ever thank him for that, at least not in this life. But I can return the favor. I can save his son from you again, and save the others who follow me, and I shall." I turned to Manteo. "I am ready to leave now."

I looked to Wanchese once more. "I hope never to see you again. And that is the truth."

I have not seen Wanchese since that meeting and, as now seems certain, shall not again. I say I am certain for I know the ships we saw today were English. How I know this, I cannot say, but I do indeed know it.

Just as I know that they will soon be back.

forty-eight

The ships are back. They arrived sometime last night. Now they are at anchor, still far offshore where the water is deep, but close enough for us to see that they are indeed English.

I am beside myself with joy. This morning, Chance and I danced together on the beach, splashing in the small waves and waving to the ships even though I knew they were too far off to see us do that.

Chance had never seen anything upon the ocean, save water and sky. The Indians only use their canoes on the wide water between these islands and the mainland.

"What, Mommy, what?" he asked, pointing.

"Ships," I said. "They are ships, my darling, and they are here to take us home."

He knows the word "home." He knitted his little brow and looked toward the village.

"No, darling, not that home. The one over there." I pointed out to sea. "The one way over there."

He smiled. I smiled. We danced. The Indians who had come down to the beach to see the ships laughed and pointed at us.

"We go," I said in their language as I pointed at the ships. "With them."

They all nodded and smiled.

Together, Chance and I danced and skipped over the great sand dunes and along the path to the village. It was time for me to find my only English dress, the one that Audry made for me. It was time to find all our things.

The ships are back. We are going home.

forty–nine

Our joy was short-lived. While Chance and I were gathering our things, a shout went up—word from the shore. Chance and I ran back to the beach. And as we watched, the ships began to make sail. All of them.

"No!" I shouted. "Where are you going? Don't leave! We are here!"

But, of course, they could not hear.

Chance was bewildered, and I fought to control myself. I told myself they might just be moving closer, that there was no point in frightening my son or myself. But my hopes were dashed when the ships did indeed sail away, as we stood watching. There were clouds gathering on the far horizon behind them, and I felt as if they had settled on me. Greatly dejected, I took Chance's hand and we turned back toward the village.

Manteo and Benginoor were standing together on the great dunes.

"A storm comes," said Manteo. "The ships will sail out to sea so they will not be pushed onto this shore. They will return. Be not sad."

Benginoor smiled in agreement. "Be not sad, Merry Moth. Be as you are—be a merry moth."

How could I not smile at her words? The ships would surely return.

But I am beginning to lose my clarity on what has truly been happening and what has occurred only in my dreams—which have been fitful, indeed. I know the storm did arrive. It lasted for three days and nights. But now it has cleared.

How soon will the ships be back?

Will they be back?

My mind is in constant turmoil. No wonder I am disoriented. Would you not be?

fifty

The ships are back again, but they have not returned here. They are to the north, at anchor outside the ocean inlet that allows entry to Roanoke. And we are all in a great quandary.

Five days ago, when two full days had passed without their return, Manteo sent men in canoes to Roanoke to see if the English had returned there. They have—but so, too, have Wanchese's men. According to Manteo's scouts, the English have been ashore on Roanoke. The scouts heard them fire their harquebus into the air and play loud English music, so they are certainly looking for the lost colony.

But the scouts said that Wanchese's men were also on the island. They were trying to drive the English away, but they dared not fight them directly. So Wanchese's men set a large blaze on one end of the island and when the English went to it in hope of finding the lost colonists, Wanchese's men hid and shot arrows at them, and then melted back into the forest. At night, they paddled to another part of the island and tried the ruse again. After three days of this, wherein the English lost several of their men to the Indian arrows, the English went back to their ships and came ashore no more. Two of Manteo's men have remained hidden in the forest on Roanoke with their canoe, to watch. If the ships set sail, say the scouts, the two men will paddle all night to return and tell us.

Manteo asked the scouts if the English had seen the signpost with "Croatoan" carved upon it, and the men answered in the affirmative. The scouts had followed their English footprints and seen many of them gathered around that signpost.

"That is good," said Manteo to me in English. "The English will come here when they give up on Roanoke."

"I do hope so," I said.

Manteo turned back to the scouts. "Did you get close enough to see any of the English?" he asked in their language.

"In their boats only," answered the lead scout. "They circle the island, calling out, making loud noises, and playing their music. Their leader is with them, one we knew from before."

I couldn't help but ask, "Which one?"

The scout pointed at me. "The tall one to which you were wife."

My heart took a turn when I heard that. Going home has been such a happy thought that I have not let my mind run to any of the trickier corners that returning to England will include. John White will be a very tricky corner, indeed. But I shall deal with that, and with him, if the time comes.

No. *When* the time comes. Manteo is right. John certainly knows where Croatoan is; a small blessing. He and the rest of the English will surely come. Simon may well be with them.

When I again pick up this quill, I expect it will be to pen a most happy page. A most happy page, indeed.

fifty-one

The ships are under sail again, and they come this way. This morning at first light, the scouts came back, shouting the news even before the bow of their canoe came ashore.

"They come!" called out the scouts. "The English are on the great water, heading this way! All of them!"

Most everyone in the village rushed over the dunes and to the beach, but I did not. Nor did Chance. I made him stay with me while I carefully changed my clothes. I put on the dress that Audry made for me and unbraided my hair, trying to remember how to pin it back up in a proper English bun. The entire time, I sang. But like Richard Tomkins so long ago with his fiddle, I found I had forgotten the tunes and the words.

It has made no difference to me, or to Chance. We are happy, in this moment, Chance because he can see how glad I am, and I because we will soon greet our fellow Englishmen.

I am now fully and properly attired. With Chance at my side, we will set out for the beach, to be reunited with our own. I think we shall skip, English style, all the way. Chance will have fun learning to do that.

So I close this journal and will carry it with me, to be opened again I know not when.

Until then.

fifty-two

I am still on Croatoan, as is Chance. I can barely bring myself to write it.

The ships did come. They appeared later that morning, three of them, all sailing south together. It was a beautiful sight. Their sails billowed white against the clear blue sky and even at the great distance, their many-colored pennants flew gaily atop their masts.

But they kept sailing.

At first, we did not realize it. We watched with happy anticipation as they appeared, then with increasing wariness as their sails remained full, and finally in stunned and confused silence as they kept sailing and slowly disappeared, still heading south.

"A storm?" I asked Manteo.

"No," he said. "No storm comes."

"What, then?"

"I do not know."

No one knew. How could we? All we knew was that the English were gone, silently vanished over a bright horizon, perhaps bound for Hispaniola and the Caykos. Away from here.

That was days ago. I have spent those days and nights here on the beach with Chance. I dared not leave, could not believe what we had seen. Of course they would come back. But they have not.

Chance and I still wait, he as naked as an Indian child and I in my English dress. The dress has become wet and sandy, heavy and grating on my skin, but I will not remove it. I must be wearing it when they return.

Manteo says they will not. It has been many days. The skies have been clear and the winds fair. If they were coming back, he says, they would have already done so.

Each day of my vigil, Benginoor and one or two of the Indian women have come down to the beach with food for us. Chance eats happily. I do not eat at all.

The nights have been warm. Chance and I sleep on the beach, his little head on my shoulder and mine on the sheaves of this journal. Though I have not truly slept. I am afraid of my dreams. I do not want any of them to be true, especially this one, that the English have not returned for us.

Of course, it's a dream. What else could it be? Why else would they have continued past? We left them a signpost, did we not? They all saw it, did they not? John White is among them. He could not abandon his fellow countrymen a second time, could he?

My head swims from lack of food and lack of sleep. I know I cannot deny myself forever. I will once again set down this quill.

It is time for this dream to end.

It is time for me to sleep.

fifty-three

This is the last page of this journal. I shall not write another.

I woke up on the beach this morning, Chance at my side. Together, we ate. And then my head began to clear. Gone were all the dreams. Gone were all the fears. I knew where I was. And I knew what I had to do.

So now Chance and I are at the water's edge. I have brought the journal with me, every sheet of it from the very beginning.

I have been reading them, starting with the first page, telling my own story only to myself, and then, as I finish each sheet, I hold it up into the wind at my back and I let it go, watching through tear-filled eyes as each page of this journal sails and flutters briefly in the wind before falling into the sea.

Chance runs after the sheets as I let them go, running to the ocean's edge as one at a time they fly away in the wind. He turns to

243

me and points as they fall into the waves to disappear like melting snowflakes. In the ankle-deep water he laughs, he dances, he shouts, "Look, Mommy! Look!"

He makes me smile in spite of myself, God love him.

God save him.

Goodbye.